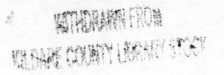

TEN DAYS

Also by Austin Duffy

This Living and Immortal Thing

Ten Days

Austin Duffy

GRANTA

Granta Publications, 12 Addison Avenue, London, W11 4QR

First published in Great Britain by Granta Books, 2021

A CIP catalogue record for this book
is available from the British Library

1 3 5 7 9 10 8 6 4 2

ISBN 978 1 78378 630 5 (hardback)
ISBN 978 1 78378 632 9 (ebook)

www.granta.com

Typeset in Garamond by Patty Rennie
Printed and bound by CPI Group (UK) Ltd, Croydon, CR0 4YY

For Naomi and Theo and Vered

'No more to say, and nothing to weep for but the Beings in the Dream, trapped in its disappearance'

from 'Kaddish' by Allen Ginsberg

PART I

I

HIS DAUGHTER CALLS him Mike. She has done ever since the age of eight or so, when it began as a precocious joke whose origin nobody can remember. But it started around the time he left the family home, so he wasn't about to get all huffy about it, to make demands he wasn't in any position to make, and it stuck. When his wife would hassle him about some small thing – like where he had been the evening before or, for that matter, an entire lost weekend – their daughter would lift her head up from her colouring book, saying, 'Yeah, Mike, where were you exactly?', adding a note of irony to what was by that stage a fairly raw antagonism. He and his wife would look at each other and come close to smiling, and for a while it wasn't clear whose side their daughter had taken.

But then it was clear, and 'Mike' disappeared from the scene and probably didn't get much of a mention during the whole period of time that followed. Those years seemed to pass as smooth and continuous as a highway, with only the odd event registering – rarely in a good way – like road signs advertising some place you've never heard of and have no desire to go to. You veer there anyway. In other words, time passed, and he always seemed to be surprised by this.

2

HIS NAME IS not Mike, or even Michael, but Wolf, as in Wolfgang. You'd think a child would relish that over the mundane alias she chose for him. Especially an English child, which Ruth was, having been born and brought up in London. But even later on, when he came back into things, the family fold et cetera, having barely seen her for the seven years of his exile, his daughter persisted with it, although now with more of an adult sensibility.

'Look at Mike, sitting at the head of the table,' she said on that first morning of his prodigal return, when she appeared at the kitchen door for breakfast and found him back in his old spot. 'Where did you sleep last night then?'

'Behave yourself,' her mother said, but she was grinning. This was one year ago.

He probably grinned also, unsure whether it bothered him or not, which it did of course. But the truth was he felt like a Mike that morning, a randomer who had insinuated himself back into things and was now encroaching with intent upon their female territory, like that recurring and most suspect of characters in the wildlife documentaries his daughter compulsively watched, the stray male.

The night before, he had flown back to London from Prague upon hearing about his wife Miriam's illness. Her brother Isaac had called him – screaming at him over the phone – and he went straight to the airport, abandoning the woman he'd gone there with. He didn't even have any luggage with him. When he arrived at Stansted he took a taxi directly to his old home. Miriam answered the door in tears and they held each other for a long time, all night in fact. Since then he had barely left her side, until two weeks ago, when she died of ovarian cancer.

'I slept in our room, if you must know,' was his reply to his daughter's question, returning her gaze with directness, figuring that the only way to deal with a teenager was head-on.

Ruth shrugged, affecting nonchalance, before coming into the kitchen to get some cereal.

3

EVEN NOW, AS she slept beside him on the aeroplane – in business class by the way – his daughter's body was twisted as far away from him as her seat would allow, in case he attempted to take advantage by sneaking in some paternal affection. Truth be told he was tempted to try. Instead, he raised his glass, asking for more champagne. Most of the other seats were empty. It was midday over the Atlantic and the cabin was filled with light.

'There you are,' the stewardess said as she filled his glass. She remained standing next to him for a second.

'You can pour her some if you'd like,' he said. 'She can have it when she wakes up.'

'Isn't she a bit young?'

He looked at his sleeping daughter.

'Yeah, I expect you're probably right.'

Ruth was in a deep sleep, or pretending to be. On her TV screen a wildlife documentary about the ice caps played. A polar bear was trying without success to catch a seal, listening with his head to the ice before jumping to his feet and hammering down his heavy paws with all his might. His frustration seemed very human. It contained the desperate realization that he would never eat again, that he would never find rest, and that this was it for him and what a fool he was to know that this day was coming all along only for it still to happen to him.

Wolf turned back to the stewardess, but she was by now at the far end of the cabin. He rested his head against the seat and stared out the window at a battlefield of small clotted clouds. They looked like they had recently been decimated by a greater force and were waiting to be absorbed into the surrounding atmosphere. The sky was light blue and homogeneous, as expansive as you can imagine.

They were on their way to New York for Rosh Hashanah, the Jewish new year, which was later than usual this year, at the beginning of October. He had booked them into the Gramercy Park Hotel until the end of the following week and the festival of Yom Kippur, the Day of Atonement. Ten days in total. They would be spending a fair bit of time with his wife's family, whom he hadn't seen in twenty years. A dinner was planned, and one or two other things. He had it all written out on an itinerary, and almost every hour of the ten days was accounted for. On the final day Ruth would go to the synagogue with the rest of the family for Yom Kippur. She was Jewish, like her mother. Meanwhile, he would wander around Manhattan, visiting some of his personal landmarks for the final time – Juilliard, which his wife Miriam was attending when they first met; the New School in Chelsea, where he transferred to complete his MFA in photography;

and most significant of all, the small apartment building in the East Village – if it still existed, and even if it didn't – where he and Miriam had married, surrounded by a group of witnesses, friends mostly, given that her family hadn't come to it. Apart from that, he would simply wander Manhattan, which he always considered to be his city, savouring in particular the nondescript parts, her wide avenues, for example, imagining that the flat earth ended at the uptown horizon, or the silent building tops and famous skyline which seemed to him always to be watching out or waiting for something. In the late afternoon he would meet Ruth and the others, once they were done with their interminable ceremony. Together they would say goodbye to his wife, scattering her ashes on the Hudson. It was one of her final wishes. She hadn't specified where exactly, simply the Upper West Side, on her birthday, which this year happened to coincide with Yom Kippur. They would find a quiet spot, away from the joggers and the rollerbladers, taking turns to scatter her ashes on the water surface. Right now, they were in an urn in the compartment above his head.

Ruth stirred, and for a brief second she looked at him with her dark, almost black eyes. It was as if they were peering at each other across the divide of species. Then her eyes closed and her breaths became visible in her shoulders as they rose and fell, in a deep sleep again. His daughter didn't know it, but this trip was for good. He hadn't even booked return flights for them. After the ceremony by the water, the final farewell to Miriam, Ruth would move in with her mother's first cousin Judy and her husband Allen. They had four children around the same age as Ruth, slightly younger and slightly older. Avram, Wolf's father-in-law, also lived with them. This was his plan, although as well as not telling Ruth any of this, he hadn't told Judy and Allen. He wanted to do that in person, to ask them – without being overly solemn about it – to look after his daughter, given that he himself would no longer be around.

4

THEY GOT INTO JFK around midday. He must have slept, as the thud of landing woke him. Ruth was sitting upright, her jacket already on, applying make-up, using her phone as a mirror. Her lips were now a clean dark red. It didn't suit her – if anything, it made her look younger.

'What?' she said.

He pretended to be looking past her out the window. Ruth stared at him for a moment, then went back to her phone-mirror. She turned to him again.

'The stewardess said you were wandering about the plane. Apparently you were mumbling to yourself again.'

Wolf avoided eye contact with her, looking instead at her screen where the wildlife documentary was on again. The polar bear was having no better luck. He seemed to be getting visibly thinner, more desperate. His fur was dirty. Probably he was out of his mind with hunger. He had made his way to some population centre where the snow was spare, revealing patches of earth. He was poking in the bins behind a supermarket. A car slowed down and then drove on. No doubt the town was used to this sort of thing. They were probably already reaching for their shotguns.

'Exactly how many drinks did you knock back, Mike?'

'Depends,' Wolf said, finally looking at his daughter. 'Are we counting Breezers?'

Ruth shook her head and went back to her phone before turning to him again.

'She asked me if you had any medical issues they needed to know about. I told her just psychiatric ones.'

He laughed.

'Did you mention my delusions of grandeur?'

'She knew about them already.'

The pilot made an announcement. It was 63 degrees. The local time was just after 1 p.m. You can't smoke until you get to the terminal. Please remain in your seats until the light goes off. Be careful with your overhead baggage. It may have moved during the flight and could cause serious injury either to you or somebody else. You can use your devices now. Thank you for travelling with United, and we hope to see you next time.

Outside, the runway was reflectant with recent rain but the sun was strong. They taxied for ages before finally docking and he could hear everyone in the economy cabin jump up to their feet to get their things. It sounded like a real melee back there and it was a relief not to be in among them. Wolf stood up to get his case from the overhead compartment. He took it down and opened it, surprised to see the urn in its see-through plastic bag. It wasn't immediately clear to him what it was and why it was there. Ruth was watching him but didn't say anything. She herself didn't have much hand luggage, just the phone and a hooded top.

5

HE WAS NOT himself a US citizen, but Ruth now was, through her mother, so he was able to accompany her through the much shorter line in immigration rather than the other one that snaked back on itself and spilt out the back of the enormous hall. It was one of the mundane tasks he had had on his list – to make sure that Ruth obtained her US passport and could stay in America indefinitely.

'Can't it wait?' she'd said to him when he broached the subject with her, only a couple of days after Miriam died. These were practically the first words they had exchanged. He needed her to go with him to the shopping centre to get the photographs taken.

'It's for your mother,' he said. 'It was one of her wishes.'

'Yes, Mike, so you've said. But can't it wait?'

'No,' he said, trying to be firm. 'She wanted me to do it straight away. In case they changed the rules or something...'

Ruth looked at him with scepticism. The back door was open, as were all the windows. The grass in their small back garden was so overgrown you could hear it rustle in the breeze. It was covered in mid-morning sun but the kitchen, where they were standing, was in cold shade. Neither of them could bear to be in the house, but neither could they bear to leave it and go out into the world which seemed to be carrying on as normal. It was one of the worst things about grief, to see how little the world noticed, the ease with which it continued and persisted, carrying on with its routines, even laughing and joking as it did so. In contrast, their house had the air of a building subject to a preservation order. They had kept it clean and functional, but it was now a historic home, some stately place where you couldn't imagine any life happening. Even the past, which the surroundings so obviously contained, appeared hard to credit, magical, a Versailles that was surely never part of the general reality. It was a relief to Wolf that in a few days the movers would come and put everything into boxes. Ruth didn't know about that either.

'Come on,' he said. 'For your mother, let's go.'

Ruth stared back at him, reduced to a frustrated silence, seeing right through his tactic. He recognized himself in her body language. A car service took them to the shopping centre. Ruth didn't say anything about that or the driver, who clearly knew Wolf well by now and said he would wait for them out front. She didn't ask why he himself wasn't driving or – come to think of it – why he hadn't driven his car in months. (His Saab was boarded up in the garage, as if it too had lost its function.) Perhaps Ruth put it down to grief, which she knew all about now.

The passport photos emerged from the machine with a whirr, a painless labour, and there she was, his daughter, in the sticky images he held in his hands. She stared back at him with a defiance whose shallow depth you could easily gauge, right down to the raw matter underneath, how inflamed and hurt it was. He didn't let the images dry properly, and all but one of them smudged, the colours running down her face. He already had the other documentation – Miriam's birth certificate and passport, Ruth's own birth cert, her UK passport, even his and Miriam's New York State marriage licence, which was not needed – and the car took them to the US embassy, where he paid the extra money to fast-track the application. Ruth's passport arrived by courier the day before they left for the States.

'What's your business here?' the JFK official was now saying to him. He held Wolf's Irish passport in the air.

'I'm accompanying my daughter. We're here for the religious holidays. The Jewish ones.'

'Shana Tova,' the official said.

'We're not Jewish. Or at least I'm not. My daughter is, technically.'

'Shana Tova,' Ruth said to the official. 'Don't mind him.'

The man stamped Wolf's Irish passport and Ruth's US one, then handed them back without saying another word.

Baggage claim was chaos. There was nothing for the longest time, and then a harsh siren sounded and the belt kicked into action. He thought something must be wrong. It spun around emptily for a few minutes before the suitcases started tumbling onto the carousel. It was terrifying, shoulders closing in on him, ready to lunge, to fight to the death if necessary. The luggage made a thumping noise as the cases landed on top of each other. They were all identical.

'What colour is it?'

The voice was Ruth's, impatient with him. She already had hers. He didn't answer her. All he wanted was to get away from here. He backed away until the pressure eased as the crowd thinned, and then was more or less absent. He was drawn towards a bright advertisement on the wall, a large family having some sort of meal, all standing looking back at him, glasses raised. He heard his name. It was Ruth, coming towards him dragging two large cases.

'Can you at least give me a hand?'

Arrivals was overwhelming, the amount of people gathered there. He stopped in his tracks, and Ruth had to come back and fetch him. What sort of place was this? At least Ruth seemed to know where to go, and she led him through the crowd and outdoors to the first gasps of fresh air. It was a relief to stand in the thick late-summer air, with its pleasant breeze. The sense of panic washed away. Luckily they didn't have to wait long for a taxi and they sat in silence looking out their windows as the car pulled out of the airport grounds. The recent rain had freshened things up and there was a sweet still-summer smell which disappeared as the windows rose and he became aware of the air conditioning. They passed through the strip malls, cemeteries, disused industrial parks, hospitals and depressing rows of wood-framed housing which comprised the Long Island and Queens suburban landscape. It could have been any urban setting, not particularly First

World. But then suddenly they were on the Triboro bridge and Manhattan was slightly below them but appearing to float upwards in the air. It was a beautiful late-September day, as clear as you can imagine. Not a cloud visible, the sky empty, simply blue, enormous.

6

'WHY CAN'T I have my own room, Mike?'

They were outside their hotel room. It was taking him an age to figure out how to open the door. 'Here, give it to me,' Ruth said, taking the card off him. There was a click and she pushed the door open and went inside towards the double bed. Turning around, she stared at him, not particularly hostile.

'I'm serious. Why can't I?'

'What?'

'Have my own room?!'

'I don't know,' he said. 'I guess I hadn't thought about it.'

It was the truth. He hadn't even checked out other hotels in the area. Miriam had always had a thing about this one – it had come up in their conversation many times down the years, symbolizing in her mind the wealthy state, although neither of them had ever stayed here. He may have even recalled an occasion from twenty years ago, when they were both living in New York and they'd gone to the rooftop bar for a drink. But the occasion was not enjoyable as Miriam had felt oppressed by the prohibitive expense of everything, while he had looked around at the other people, full of envy that it was them and not him who clearly had it all.

His daughter was still facing him, her hands by her sides, balled into fists. She had a point. They had never previously shared a room, or at least not since she was a couple of months old.

'Is that the done thing?' he said. 'I mean, at your age?'

Ruth let out an exaggerated groan.

'I can check tomorrow at reception,' he said, 'about getting another room. I'll ask them what age you have to be, legally I mean. What their regulations are.'

She was ignoring him now and threw herself onto the double bed. After a minute she sat up and took off her boots, then climbed under the covers. He sat on the edge of the small single bed across from her, looking at her shape as it steadily rose and fell. He remembered very clearly holding her in his arms when she was just hours into her life, premature, barely bigger than his hand. She had turned yellow and the doctors were debating whether light therapy was needed. He made a soft bedding out of his jacket and jumper, and laid her on the windowsill of the hospital room. The nurses had found it funny. The UV rays don't penetrate the glass, you know. But still he persisted.

It was soon apparent that Ruth was asleep. He waited for a while before going over and pulling the curtains to make it dark for her. For a long time he stood peering out the window through the gap at the side. There was no view, just the aspect of the adjacent building pressed right up against them. He could have been anywhere staring at the opaque and featureless concrete, Miriam on the bed behind him sleeping soundly. Vilnius perhaps, that trip they took once. When was that? Mir had wanted to explore her roots. The purring noise reminded him of her presence. His wife always snored when she slept. It was all or nothing with her. If she wasn't snoring her head off she was wide awake, her nose buried in a book, up till all hours. He turned and watched her shape rising and falling. For some reason they'd been given a twin room. Two beds. These hotels on the edge of Europe. You took what you were given with them. Tomorrow they would go to the memorial in the forest. Strange that he had a memory of it ahead of time, as if it had already happened. He could picture the scene in its entirety. The rain strengthening, they stood not far from those large indentations in the earth. He left Miriam and walked over to face the forest, which seemed to extend forever into its own silence. An impenetrable mesh. The forest frightened him. Europe's memory was contained in those gnarled trees, perhaps even her soul in their blackened roots. The same trees present since the time of Christ, a persistence of the Dark Ages right there in front of him. God knows how long he stood there. Looking out at the opaque and featureless concrete, it was timeless, utterly timeless.

7

FROM THE TOP floor of the hotel he looked out at a Manhattan covered by a morning mist. Night was in the process of passing, the remnant of dark seeming to cling to the buildings, many of which still had their lights on. He was in an outdoor terraced area enclosed by a perimeter wall that he could just about see over. It was unclear whether the restaurant was even open yet. The tables were set up for service, but nobody was about. The only other people were two men in tuxedos sitting at one of the outside tables, their ties loose, a bottle of champagne in front of them in a bucket. The air had a chill to it. It came as a surprise when a waiter – who just before had walked by, putting on his tie – approached Wolf bearing a cup of coffee on an unnecessary tray. Wolf took it and thanked him, then stood looking over the wall as he sipped from it. The men in tuxedos were laughing but he couldn't make out what they were saying. It sounded like Russian. Their speech was slurred. They looked over at Wolf when his phone rang.

'How's Rosh Hashanah with the in-laws?'

It was Maurice, Wolf's solicitor back in London. Wolf had been expecting the call – it was the first item on today's agenda in his itinerary for the day. He knew enough not to let the notebook out of his sight. Maurice's voice was small and distant, and Wolf could tell that he had him on speaker phone, was probably driving.

'Have you owned up to all your imperfections then, Wolfgang? Promised to do better?'

Wolf laughed. Maurice himself was Jewish but he came from a secular wealthy family. His wife was Japanese. When you went around to their house you had to take your shoes off and sit on cushions on the floor.

'The Islington property is with the management company,' Wolf said, all business, his notebook open in front of him. 'They have your details. I've also opened an account here in Ruth's name, apparently.'

'Apparently?'

'Have you got a pen?'

'My, you've been a busy boy. Hold on a sec, will you?'

It was a while before Maurice spoke again. Classical music played on the stereo system of his car, and it was pleasant listening to it while looking out at a smouldering Manhattan coming to life, changing by the second in increments that were difficult to quantify, no matter how hard Wolf stared at the mist emanating from the backs of the buildings, the hazy sky yet to reveal itself, street noise becoming more appreciable from far below, another day on earth. Hard to believe he was down to his final few. Every now and again Maurice made some guttural noises of frustration, a reminder that he was on the other end, and Wolf could visualize him looking about his person for a pen, a scrap of paper.

'I had to pull in,' Maurice said then, still on speaker.

He let out a loud sigh to calm himself. 'All right. Shoot.'

Wolf said nothing. He was looking at the sky. In his hand was a piece of paper, an official-looking letter addressed to him in a small font.

'The account number, my friend?' the voice in his ear said.

Wolf called out the bank account number and sort code.

'Half of everything goes in there,' he said, again all business. It was as if somebody was speaking on his behalf. 'The rest goes into the trust.'

Neither of them spoke for a while, and Wolf could hear Maurice as he arranged his papers, followed then by the sound of a zip. His solicitor was surprisingly well organized, even fastidious in certain ways, which for sure was at odds with your initial impressions of him, his garrulousness and the fact that he was constantly in piss-taking mode. They had known each other, what, fourteen, fifteen years? Dating from the time Miriam and he had minor legal trouble with their neighbour over a botched heating job they had had inserted. For a spell Miriam and he were waking in a smoke-filled bedroom. When she mentioned that to Maurice at the first consultation he said, 'Please now, no marital particulars,' and laughed. Miriam thought he was untrustworthy and not very professional, but Wolf liked him and he ended up doing a good job for them.

A car beeped in the background.

'OH PISS OFF!' Maurice shouted. 'People have no patience any more, Wolfgang. Fucking zero.'

'I bet your arse is hanging out though.'

There was a delay.

'Maybe a tad,' Maurice said, and they both laughed. Maurice was a hopeless driver. He tended to make sudden lurches with the car, often without looking, and had very little spatial awareness. It was an uncomfortable experience to get into a vehicle with him. The classical music was to calm his road rage. His wife's idea. He didn't otherwise listen to it.

'Is the guardianship sorted?' he asked.

'It hasn't been discussed yet,' Wolf said. 'At least as far as I can remember.'

'Which reminds me,' said Maurice, 'you going to look up that ex-girlfriend of yours when you're there? What's her name again, Debbie ... Debs, you know, the one you left high and dry in Prague? I always had a bit of a thing for her ...'

Wolf didn't say anything.

'Come on,' Maurice said, 'don't tell me you've deleted that nice bit of memory. Not sure if I told you, but she's hit the big time. Ichika's on the mailing list for her blog that she still puts out. She's in something off-Broadway. Doing well, apparently. You should look her up. Or on second thoughts, maybe not.'

Maurice laughed, then changed the subject.

'The St James's Street gallery want to extend terms,' he said.

Wolf didn't know what he was referring to, but wasn't inclined to say so. 'Has anything sold?'

'They have *overseas interest* ... apparently.'

Maurice yawned and Wolf could sense a collapse in his friend's energy levels. He was prone to these spasms of exhaustion, sudden apathy, which could happen at any time.

Maurice himself put it down to fluctuating blood sugar. Wolf could picture him sitting in his Merc, jutting out in the lane of traffic, cars having to make allowance for him, his large frame slumped over in the low seat, glasses off, rubbing at his eyes. He would take himself off for a pastry now, and a double espresso.

'The plan is still the plan?' Maurice said then.

'The plan is still the plan.'

'Pity,' Maurice said, recovering his energy. 'They want to do another ECM thing. Another retrospective, or whatever, of all the stuff they've used for their cover art down the years ... more or less as a tribute to Barbara Wojirsh, who – I keep forgetting – is she still alive? Or has she popped her clogs and trotted off to some minimalist Valhalla in the sky?'

Wolf laughed.

'Anyway,' Maurice continued, 'they want to include you obviously, and one or two others ... Lars has been in touch. He said he emailed you but no reply.'

'I don't know,' Wolf said.

'I can put in a clause that releases those pieces. The new stuff. To the James's people, I mean. They're pure lowball anyway, those prices ... That was on me, that one. A mistake.'

There was silence for a while. Maurice must have thought Wolf was thinking over what he'd said. But he wasn't, he was simply looking out at Manhattan and had barely been following what Maurice was saying. The mist was now tinged with yellow and the sun was threatening to burst through. He drank some of his coffee.

'Your value will increase, you know?'

Wolf laughed, but then realized Maurice was being at least half serious.

'It's a natural law, Wolfgang. Practically Newtonian. Supply and demand, my son. Supply and demand.'

Wolf laughed out loud.

'Lars thinks you should be the "moral centre" of the thing this time. The retrospective.'

Lars. The name was familiar. Wolf laughed anyway. In any case, he could picture the conversation, Maurice sitting in front of someone with his steak and Scotch, agreeing with everything, *you're absolutely right, my son, one hundred facking per cent*, his mouth full of food.

'Lars thinks or you think?' Wolf said.

'A meeting of minds, Wolfgang, a meeting of minds!'

They both laughed, after which there was some more silence.

'The plan is still the plan,' Wolf said then.

He hung up and stood, finishing his coffee, looking out at the downtown skyline. The sun was now coating it in gold. If you photographed it, it would be pure kitsch, the type of thing he hated most, art he would never do himself in a million years. But it was very beautiful. He felt slightly weakened all of a sudden, ridiculous really, but there it was: the beauty of the scene overwhelmed him, and he was aware that he was using his arms to support himself. The sensation passed and he was able to straighten himself. He finished the dregs of his coffee and walked out past the two Russian-speaking men. One of them raised his open hand to him in greeting as if he knew him.

8

'SO WHAT DO you want to do today then?'

She ignored him, so he had to repeat the question.

'Nothing,' Ruth said, not looking up from her phone.

'Well we have to do something.'

When she did look up for a split second it was Miriam's face staring back at him. The reddish tint to Ruth's hair, it was all Mir, her complexion darker than normal in the light they were sitting in. He didn't want to move an inch in case she disappeared.

'I told you already,' she said. 'I've got plans.'

The waitress came to their table. It was strange because she acted as if she knew them. She said that the breakfast specials were the same as yesterday. Will we start you on some drinks? She looked at Wolf. Black coffee, right? She looked at Ruth. Soy milk for you, right?

'I'll just have some seltzer thanks,' Ruth said.

The waitress said she'd give them a few minutes for food.

She must have mixed them up with some other father and daughter. He had never set foot in this place before. He wanted to say something to Ruth but decided against it. Instead he looked down at his menu, but it was hard to make sense of it. The silence between him and Ruth made the background noise louder – three women sitting next to them, a business man with his small child, agitated, trying to stop her from climbing out of her high chair. The waitress attended to the three women. Something was said and they all laughed. The waitress walked away. The back of her shirt was torn slightly. A strand of it glided free and loose, following after her in a playful buoyancy as she crossed the room. Ruth was looking at him.

'You do realise, don't you, Mike,' she said, 'that they know when you're checking them out like that?'

'And who's to say she wasn't giving me the eye?'

'Only because you were staring at her.'

'I'm nineteen in here, you know,' and he tapped the side of his head.

'Yeah, well treble it.'

He laughed. His daughter looked back at her phone. In her downward face he got another glimpse of Miriam. But then Ruth moved and the likeness vanished. He looked around the restaurant. In the booth across from them was a man dressed head to toe in leather. Whatever bare skin was visible was tattooed. Multiple piercings. The more he looked at the man the more detail he noticed. Leather bandana. He even had a leather collar around his neck and thick leather bracelets around his lower arms.

Wolf looked at Ruth and nodded in the man's direction.

'What?' Ruth said, and he gave her a minute to observe the man before leaning into the table.

'Leather underpants too, I'd say.'

Ruth acted irritated but then she couldn't help herself and laughed.

'Or maybe he's wearing his little boy pants,' he said. 'What do you reckon? Spiderman ones?'

Ruth laughed again.

'I'd say he's more of a Batboy,' she said, and for just a minute there was no tension between them and they sat like any other father daughter. A waiter came with a tray and put some food in front of them. Wolf didn't recall ordering anything. Ruth seemed unsurprised.

'When are we seeing your family?' he asked her. 'Avram and . . . the other ones.'

'*The other ones?*'

'It's today right?'

'They're your family too you know.'

'Allen and Judy,' he said, relieved that the names came to him. She was looking at him again, considering something.

'It must be awkward for you all the same though, Mike,' she said, 'seeing them after all these years. After what you did.'

'Jesus Christ, Ruth.'

'Well, for starters, you'd better not mention *him*.'

He laughed.

He looked directly at her. She had turned to face out to the restaurant, but he persisted in looking at her, until she finally couldn't ignore the burn of his gaze.

'What?'

'How long are you going to keep calling me that?'

A tinge of colour came into her face.

'What else am I supposed to call you? Dad?'

He laughed. That tone of hers again. He had always found his daughter to be very funny, more than the average, right back to when she was very small. He laughed again, properly this time.

'What?!' Ruth said, but then she started to laugh also and for the second time in a matter of minutes he saw that she had forgotten about her mother. Then she abruptly stopped and looked downwards. She could as easily start to cry.

The waitress brought him a refill of coffee. After she left he leaned into the table to Ruth.

'How's the love life? Any boys I should know about?'

'Jesus Christ!'

'I thought we weren't supposed to mention him.'

She ignored him. His question had been at least semi-serious though. With Ruth there had never been any mention of boyfriends. It had crossed his mind more than once that she might be gay. Not that that would bother him. If anything it would come as an enormous relief. At one swoop most of the danger in the world would not apply to her. The violent little house generals with their moods and private kingdoms. At least he hadn't been one of those. He put his coffee down and smiled at her as she was taking up her drink.

'Or girls?' he said.

Ruth inhaled her seltzer so that some of it came out her nose, causing her to cough and splutter.

'Fuck sakes!' she said.

She bent right over, coughing some more to clear her throat. People looked over at them.

'Stop it, will you?' she said, her voice still thin from coughing.

'What?' Wolf said, after Ruth had recovered.

'This! Being all, I don't know, parental.'

'Well it is my job.'

She looked at him as if this horrifying fact had struck her for the first time.

'Yeah, well stop it.'

The waitress asked if everything was all right. Wolf took up his coffee and Ruth leaned into her oatmeal, and he knew that she was thinking of her mother.

9

THERE MUST HAVE been a visit to the bank. In his bag there was a folder with the Citi logo on it. He took it out and went through the contents. It seemed to contain mostly junk, promotional material, but then he saw that there were also details of the account he had opened in Ruth's name. He'd lodged $865,000, give or take, in it, the proceeds from the recent sale of his apartment in London, the one he had bought after initially separating from Miriam all those years ago. It had gone up in price in the intervening years, almost doubled. It turned out that separating from his wife for those years had been a sound business decision. Plus he'd made good money in recent years, ridiculous money considering what he did for a living – taking photographs, for record companies, magazines, or as original artwork, enhancing them digitally using technical skills that anyone could learn these days, but in fairness had been pretty innovative at one time. And he did have an eye for the striking, with the good sense to be as ambiguous as possible, leaving things mostly open to interpretation. He put the folder back in the bag and placed the bag on the floor. Where was she anyway? How long had he been waiting here? It felt like a long time, possibly all afternoon. He took out his notebook. Each page had its own daily itinerary, the preceding days crossed off. There was nothing in it about where she might be. The manager had already been over to ask if 'sir' was OK. He felt a nervousness, an agitation, ratcheting up inside him. She should tell him where she was going, and when to expect her back. The manager came over again.

'Can I get you another coffee?'

'No thanks,' Wolf replied.

He watched after the man as he went back behind his desk at reception. Some people approached the desk. There was a bag down at Wolf's feet. He took it up on his lap, opened it. Bank stuff. He removed a blue and white folder with the Citi logo on it. Mostly it contained junk promotional material, but also in the folder were details of the account which clearly he had opened in Ruth's name. He had lodged $865,000 in it, give or take, proceeds from the sale of his apartment, the one he had bought after initially separating from Miriam all those years ago. It had gone up in price in the intervening years, almost doubled actually.

He looked up and saw Ruth outside. That was his daughter, he recognized her straight away. She was talking to someone outside the hotel, an older woman wearing a scarf over her hair. It was clear from their body language that they knew each other well. Ruth was relaxed, she even laughed once or twice. They embraced and the woman stepped into the car that they were standing beside. Ruth watched as she drove off. Then she turned and came through the revolving doors, her face set firm again. She saw Wolf and came over to him.

'Where have you been?'

He must have shouted at her because the manager and the other people at the desk looked over at him. Ruth noticed this also. She walked towards him, but stopped some distance from him. His daughter had a fear of 'scenes'. It was one of the only advantages he had over her. He noticed that she was wearing make-up, and a relatively nice blouse, black obviously, but still, dressed for an occasion. She was never going to answer his question. Her black eyes were fixed on him, that divide of species again.

'Who was that woman?'

Her eyes went beyond him for a second. Then she came over and sat down in the armchair opposite him. Flopped right down into it as if she had suddenly lost all of her energy. He had to repeat the question.

'You know who she is, Mike,' she said.

'Well let's assume I've forgotten.'

Ruth let out a sigh.

'Ingrit. My friend in Brooklyn, from the kibbutz two summers ago. I told you all this, that I was going to visit her. She ended up bringing me to her schul. It was miles away.'

He looked at her, neither of them saying anything. Ruth forced a smile.

'Shall we get going then?' she said.

He had an urge to shout at her. It came out of nowhere,

the desire to scream at the top of his voice. He was practically shaking with anger, but he had no idea why. He didn't even know what it was they were late for. The manager was both looking at them and pretending not to notice.

And now they were outside. The breeze was warm and strong, a little moist with rain. For a second he simply stood in it with his eyes closed. The thick warmth of the air came as a surprise and he sensed it had been a long time since he'd been outdoors. The flash of anger dissipated just as quickly as it had flared up. He was breathing deeply, noisily through the nose, as if someone had instructed him to do so. The trees of Gramercy in front of them were in the throes of a vigorous dance, a perfect frantic rhythm. Ruth was standing next to him, facing in the same direction. The tilt of her shoulders, all the weight on the right-hand side, one of Miriam's gestures. It was as if his wife was standing right there next to him. He stared at her as if she had appeared out of nowhere. But another slight shift in posture and she was gone.

Ruth started walking and he followed her, out of the sheltered area of Gramercy and in the direction of Third Avenue. They passed a loud bar before hitting a long, relatively quiet stretch leading to the busy part of the avenue blinking in the distance. At the corner he caught up with her.

'Let's get a cab,' she said, coming to a stop. Before he had a chance to reply she had stepped onto the street with her arm out.

'I wanted to show you the subway system.'

A cab was already pulling in. Ruth held the door open.

'You keep saying that.'

He ducked under her arm and got in.

'Where to?' the driver asked, making eye contact with Wolf in his mirror. Wolf stared back at him, and for a second their eyes were locked together, challenging each other. Ruth made a frustrated noise and leaned across so that her own face now appeared in the driver's mirror. Brooklyn, she said, loudly. Prospect Heights, she added. She sat back against the black leather, turning fully away from Wolf. It took them a while in heavy traffic to get onto the FDR and down to the Brooklyn Bridge, but once they reached the highway, traffic was light and they glided along with the other cars in silence, their dashboards lit up, the faces of the drivers peaceful and in their own worlds. Both of them looked out the window at Manhattan's eastern skyline, the buildings not themselves distinguishable, just an array of lights, a vast interconnected structure, like a galaxy viewed from the side. They passed over the Brooklyn Bridge. At Ruth's behest Wolf took out his phone, and Ruth entered a number on it before passing the phone back to him. A woman's voice spoke in his ear. Hello?

Ruth must have seen the look of confusion on his face.

'It's Judy,' she said, but then she took the phone back off him. We're on our way, she said. Sorry to be running late. No, actually it was all her fault. She'd been in Queens all afternoon. Then she mentioned someone called Ingrit. He looked over at her. Ingrit, she repeated into the phone. Her friend from Israel. It was the first he'd heard about it.

The name didn't mean anything to him. But whoever this Ingrit person was, she had apparently wanted to show Ruth her schul.

10

IT WAS A long time since Wolf had last seen his wife's family. Even in the years before separating from Miriam there hadn't been much contact. He and Miriam had moved to London six months after their wedding. Miriam had gone back to New York several times, but he never accompanied her. There was always some reason for him not to go, a project that needed his attention, or an event that he didn't want to miss, an opening or party, and anyway, it wasn't as if they were overly eager to see him. Although Miriam's family weren't from one of the stricter Orthodox communities who made up the part of Queens she grew up in, neither were they a million miles off it. Modern Orthodox was the term, although it was difficult to discern what was so modern about it. Her father Avram kept a kosher house. Two stoves in the kitchen. Separate utensils, plates, bowls, whatever, for the dairy and the meat in order – apparently – to abide by one of the injunctions contained in the Torah. Something about not boiling a young goat in its mother's milk, in Deuteronomy, or maybe it was one of the other ones. There seemed to be an injunction against absolutely everything. Miriam's kitchen growing up had by the sounds of things been a minefield of potential affronts to Yahweh, especially when her mother was alive, who, by all accounts, had been hardcore. She was the one who ensured the laws of kashrut were stringently adhered to, that only those animal species were consumed which had cloven hooves and were capable of chewing the cud, and had had the good fortune to have been slaughtered in the proper ritual manner, a single cut across the throat to a precise depth, severing both carotids, the jugulars, the vagus nerves, trachea, the oesophagus, certainly no higher than the epiglottis and no lower than where the cilia begin inside the throat. Miriam would recount all of this to him with an air of disbelief from the vantage point of their heathen home, but also with some nostalgia, some wistfulness, and it was clear that part of her missed the complexity which Torah adherence had lent to even the simplest thing. The lack of volition, which was liberating in its own way, and the sense of community of course, suffocating though it was a lot of the time. Obviously *they* didn't approve of him. It wasn't necessarily personal. Although everything that happened later, the separation, his infidelities, et cetera, only reinforced how right they had been all along about him, where Wolf *in absentia* really did assume the role of one of the biblical archetypes – the cautionary tale, the parable, the paradigmatic stray path that awaits any errant Jew. Miriam increased the regularity of her trips back to New York, going two or even three times a year, taking Ruth with her, all of this continuing right up to when she began chemotherapy, by which time Wolf was now back in the picture. And then, on top of everything, of course, there was the fact of the cremation itself, which really he couldn't be blamed for. Here he was merely following Miriam's very specific wishes.

There was no getting around it, it was what she wanted and she could not have been any clearer. No matter that it was very much against the Jewish tradition, where they believed in the necessity of retaining the corpse's physical integrity for when the Messiah eventually decides to show up and put everyone out of their misery, finally bringing an end to their millennia of patient waiting and suffering. Miriam had told him once about a particular burial site in Jerusalem which was hard to get into, quite competitive actually, the spots in particularly high demand being those on an incline, which will have the advantage of gravity when the end of days comes, allowing the bodies of the newly risen dead to roll down the hill towards the Rapture. They will be the first to touch the hem of the Messiah's white robe, the first to feel the power of the light emanating from Him which will melt the eyes of the gentiles, Wolf himself included, of course. None of which is possible if you are just a pile of ashes that has been strewn upon the wind and the water.

'What are you mumbling about?' Ruth was staring at him. 'You were muttering away to yourself. And, like, twitching. You nervous or something?'

'No. Not at all. Why would I be?'

Ruth looked out her window.

'I am,' she said.

The reflection of the passing scenery played on her face. Wolf looked at it, regretting his own lack of candour.

'They're going to be talking about her,' she said, and she bit into her lip.

He looked down to see her bare hand splayed out on the leather seat beside him. It was a child's hand, pure white against the black, like something frozen. He put his own hand down next to it, the barest of skin contact. It wasn't much of a gesture but it calmed him and he found it easy to imagine that the same was true for her. The car hummed along and they sat in perfect peace. If it had taken another hour to get to their destination it would have been perfectly fine by him. But by now they had arrived in Brooklyn and it was clear that they were close. There was a familiarity to the route. Ruth moved her hand away and the sense of peace vanished. He looked out the window, vaguely recognizing where he was despite the clear and obvious changes to the neighbourhood, the gentrification that he had read about. He'd always thought Brooklyn was a bit of a dump, but apparently everyone wanted to live there now. They arrived at the area where Judy and Allen lived, and which Wolf also vaguely recognized. The driver went slowly, looking for the exact address, producing a torch to look through his window at the house numbers on the old brownstones, many of which were hidden in darkness or behind overgrown bushes.

'It's just down a bit more,' Ruth said, leaning forward to speak through the small gap in the Plexiglas. Wolf had forgotten that she had been here before. The cab driver pulled in and stopped the meter, and for a few seconds nobody moved.

'What's the matter with you?' Ruth said to Wolf.

He looked at her, at a complete loss.

'What?'

'Eh, you have to pay the fare perhaps?'

He had his wallet in his hand, but he was moving too slowly for Ruth. She took it and removed some notes.

'Here. Keep the change,' she said, handing them to the driver. They got out of the car, and as they walked up the path the front door opened and Judy was standing there. Wolf hung back a little, allowing Ruth to go forward on her own.

11

A LOT OF people were gathered in the hallway to greet them. They were mostly young people, the children of Judy and Allen, but there were extras, boyfriends and girlfriends, as well as adults whom he didn't recognize. The crowd gave way and it was as if they were standing back to allow him to fall forward onto the ground. He felt a hand around his wrist and his name being called. It was Judy – he recognized her without any prompting. For a second they stood looking at each other and he wasn't sure what would happen next, but then she pulled him towards her into a strong embrace. A sense of relief coursed through him. She patted him on his back, her wiry hair against the side of his face, and he stood awkwardly holding her, rocking slightly from side to side. Judy was Miriam's first cousin. Growing up, they had always been close, more like sisters. She released Wolf from her embrace and turned back to Ruth, who was surrounded by people. He drifted to the periphery of the crowd. The children were looking at him and he sensed that his arrival had been much anticipated by them, as if he was some ghoul from lore they were finally seeing. They must have been disappointed to find him normal in appearance, no animal fur or hooves, or at least not as far as they could see. He moved over to where a group of adults were standing, old family friends and neighbours, he presumed. He had forgotten how all-inclusive these Jewish holiday celebrations were, so drastically different from his own small Christmas dinners growing up, where he would sit silently with his parents, without music, and even without much in the way of television, which for them was limited to the Irish channels, before his father would disappear into the garage to work on the old motors he used to pick up and repair as a hobby while listening to German radio on long wave. Both Wolf's parents were German. His father had come to Dublin for a job with Aer Lingus with a plan to stay for just three or four years, but they ended up remaining there until their deaths, his father's occurring suddenly while Wolf was still in school, and his mother's twenty years ago now, from Alzheimer's, a condition she had feared all her life, given that it had occurred in her own father and in others in the family. Our plague, she called it. 'Shoot me when I also get it.' He still felt slightly guilty that he didn't do as she had asked, especially as there was no way to gauge her suffering. He had no clue really, not even a notion about it, even though he made an effort to see her more or less semi-regularly and fulfilled all the duties required of him as the son and only child. But you only ever have the surface to go by – you can have no honest idea even at the best of times about another being's consciousness, much less one whose brain has been hollowed out like hers had been, but which was doubtless still capable of inflicting upon her a daily torture, barely lessened by sleep, which, according to the attendants, she did little of, or by the drugs, the sedatives et cetera, which they seemed to shovel into her and to which she was pretty resistant. She was full time by that stage. A falls risk, according to the home assessment. His mother was just a corpse really, sitting in a chair with her wispy hair and bulging eyes. She had no idea who he was, and the visits he made to see her were pointless. All of which is to say that none of this would happen to him.

In the adjacent room he got a glimpse of Avram, his father-in-law, sitting in an armchair, sleeping. Instead of going to him he turned to observe Ruth, the reluctant star of the show, the focus of all the attention. Judy had her arms around her neck and was looking into her face, openly crying.

'When I look at you I see her,' Judy said, more than once. Ruth didn't know how to hold herself or react. She simply stood there, more embarrassed than anything. Wolf turned away and stood at the entrance to the room where Avram was dozing. He went over and stood in front of the old man, observing him for a moment – the chest rising and falling, a slight whistling snore. It was like standing in front of some dozing beast that could tear you limb from limb if it woke. An image came to him fully formed. Avram, a couple of decades younger, fat, his enormous back covered in thick hair. He was sitting on the edge of a swimming pool. It must have been some family event, during the early days of his and Miriam's relationship. The look of contempt Avram gave Wolf as he approached to say hello. He shook Wolf's hand before turning and sliding into the water, like a creature born to it, gliding with incredible fluidity along the bottom of the pool before resurfacing on the far side a few seconds later. Now Avram stirred, sensing a presence in front of him. He opened his eyes and stared up at Wolf, briefly at a loss. Wolf braced himself. There was nothing delicate about his father-in-law, and Wolf would not have been surprised if the old man started shouting at him, shaken by some unspecified rage, before charging at him with fists and a lowered head. But there was none of that. If anything, Avram seemed unsure of who it was standing there, and Wolf ignored the impulse to prompt him.

'Ah ... W–Wolfgang,' the old man said then, holding his head back at an angle as if he was trying to see around the edge of a cataract.

'It's OK. Sit,' Wolf said, seeing his father-in-law struggle to get to his feet. But Avram ignored him, and something stopped Wolf from going to him and helping him up. Avram was old now, and Wolf was registering this for the first time. He must have been well into his eighties. So shrunken, it would take nothing to push him over onto the ground and keep him there, to stand over him and not let him up, until all he could do was lie there in submission. Wolf watched him as he slowly straightened up. He took a step towards Wolf and put out his hand, which trembled badly. Wolf looked at it before shaking it. The rough skin, the still-tight grip came as a surprise. There was a time when Avram, a force of nature in his day, would stand in front of you and block out all the light. All you knew was his presence, his demands and his moods, even if his speech was a bit muddled and thickly accented, English being his second language, and a distant second one at that. Now when he stepped back and looked at Wolf his gaze seemed only to be partially taking him in, and the steadiness of it had been replaced by a flickering. Wolf felt taller than him for the first time, though in actual fact he had always been the much taller man.

'You're looking well,' Wolf said.

It wasn't true, but he was nicely dressed and it was clear that the old man was being well minded by his niece Judy. He looked the part of the perfectly benign grandfather, and it almost made it hard for Wolf to locate the rancour between them. They stood in silence. In any case, most of the house's energy was concentrated in the hallway where the young were. In here it was just old men.

'In Yiddish we have expression,' Avram said. 'Weeds don't die. You say this also in England?'

Wolf ignored him and instead looked around the room, whose walls were extensively covered by children's paintings, every single one of them framed, though they were nothing more than coloured scribbles. There were also photographs of Judy, Allen and various combinations of the extended family, as well as much older ones in black and white of children dressed doll-like in the costumes of their day and which had been taken in Russia – where Judy's mother Rose had come from in the early 1900s – and Lithuania, from where the parents of Avram and his brother Lenny, Judy's father, had fled to Israel, or British Palestine as it was then, to escape the Nazis in the 1940s. The room was smaller than Wolf remembered. The large table had been extended by the addition of other smaller tables at both ends and the whole thing had been set for what appeared to be at least twenty, maybe even thirty, people.

'Is that my daughter?' Avram said, noticing the plastic bag Wolf was carrying.

Wolf looked down, surprised to see that he was carrying the urn with him, its pattern visible through the plastic bag. He had no recollection of having brought it from the hotel. Perhaps Ruth had given it to him.

'It didn't seem right to leave her in the hotel.'

He handed it to Avram.

Avram took the urn from the bag, letting the bag itself fall to the ground. He held the urn out from him and, closing his eyes, spoke some words in Hebrew. He looked up at his son-in-law.

'I cannot believe my little girl is in here,' he said. He looked at the ground and Wolf thought he was going to cry, but instead there was a burst of anger.

'I did not want this,' he said, and stamped his foot.

At first Wolf thought he was referring to Miriam's death in general, but then Avram said, 'This... this is not what we do,' and it was clear he was talking about the cremation. There was disgust in his voice. Avram held the urn away from himself, but after a minute he brought it close to him and kissed it and placed it on the mantelpiece.

'I'm sorry you didn't get to see her,' Wolf said.

Avram shrugged.

'God's will.'

Wolf stared at the back of Avram's head, feeling a rush of the old hostility. If Avram even noticed, he ignored him as he took his time arranging the urn on the mantelpiece, moving another object out of the way to make room for it. Wolf stood and watched him for what felt like several minutes. Eventually Avram turned around as if he was forcing himself to look at Wolf. Neither man backed down and Wolf felt his mind to be clear. He could remember anything, at any time.

'You fly first class or economy?'

'We got upgraded.'

'Upgrade,' said Avram. 'Very nice. What about the hotel? Did you get a deal? Judy, she tell you, right, that I know the owner? Many years, a friend of mine. He owes me a lot actually. His son is the manager there.'

Wolf ignored him again and simply walked over to look at some of the photos on the wall. In several of them Miriam gazed out at him as a child. Her decency and sheer good nature were always obvious in photographs, but they were most obvious of all in photos of her from when she was very young. He found it almost unbearable to look at them and moved instead towards a large window that looked out, he now remembered, onto the garden, which was always overgrown, never used even in summer, and sunken one floor down below the level of the front of the house. The buildings across the way must have been empty because their lights did not show up in the dark glass through which he was looking, and which revealed nothing but the dense night outside and his own reflection in the ether of the window. Behind him he could see his father-in-law looking at him without any expression that he could make out. Then Avram appeared uncertain and looked around him and once more was a very old man. Ruth appeared in the dark reflection of the window to greet her grandfather. In the window's mirror she was the image of Miriam, and Avram took her into his arms. More figures appeared in the dark glass and the voices became louder as the room filled. Wolf had the feeling that he was standing in this exact spot some other time, years earlier, the decades collapsing into seconds, others crowding the reflection, Miriam especially, who would come now and check on him. He closed his eyes and could hear her voice, her breath on his cheek.

'I wanted to make sure you were surviving,' she says to him. 'These Jewish family things can be intense,' and then she laughs and again he notices how beautiful she is and how her beauty is both indistinguishable from her kindness and enhanced by it.

'It's been a long trip for you.'

He turned around. It was Allen, Judy's husband, whom Wolf recognized without any difficulty. Allen was wearing a woollen jumper despite the warm evening, and his thick beard and hair had an unkempt quality.

'It's been a long trip for you, Wolfgang,' he said again, more firmly, and Wolf returned to himself and the present. Allen hadn't changed much in the intervening years. Even his clothes seemed to be the exact ones he would have worn when Wolf had last seen him, a lifetime ago. They stood facing each other in the slightly awkward silence.

'Yes,' Wolf said then. 'It has been a journey. As they say.'

12

RUTH WAS SEATED down among the other teenagers, near Avram at the head of the table. Wolf wouldn't have been able to put a name to any of them. His daughter was quiet and he could easily sense her discomfort and awkwardness, the fact that she would literally rather be anywhere else. He recognized his own body language in hers, its stiltedness, the rigidity with which she sat. She was dressed all in black, although a little more formally than usual. Ruth was never one for bright colours, she especially hated pink. Growing up, there was no princess infatuation or playing with dolls or much in the way of any other nonsense. Any old T-shirt would do for her, more recently with some death metal band, whatever that was, on the front. The only exception to this was her full, thick hair, which she took pride in maintaining. It was a very rich dark colour whose length always surprised Wolf on the rare occasions he saw it unfurled to its full dimensions and, especially in certain light, it had that tint of red to it, the only incontrovertible residue of Miriam. He was always on the lookout for that residue, wishing it were more. Unfortunately his daughter mostly took after him in terms of her physical appearance.

Avram stood and gave a rambling speech welcoming everyone to the celebration of Rosh Hashanah, the New Year and
a time for thinking ahead and remembering. In particular,
he wanted to welcome Ruth, who had journeyed so far to
be here with her family, a word Avram emphasized. She was
mortified that everyone was now looking at her. No mention
was made of Wolf, but this was fine by him. Avram went
on to speak about those who were missing, and the silence
was sudden and unbearable. Avram wanted to say a blessing for Miriam, and everyone had to hold hands. Wolf held
the hands of the two people on either side of him, one of
the younger children and, on his right side, a middle-aged
woman whom he didn't know and who held his hand very
limply, their skin barely making contact. Everyone except
Wolf began to murmur in Hebrew. He looked over at Ruth's
downturned face and was surprised to see that she seemed
to be reciting the prayer. She had been going to Hebrew
school in London once a week since about the age of eight
or nine, but he had never seen any outward evidence of
this before and he had always thought it just a social club.
But now here she was, eyes closed, mouthing what appeared
to him to be perfect Hebrew. Avram's voice rose above
everyone else's and it was alternately steady and thick, then
hoarse and thin. There were glimpses of his old power in the
voice, the physical force that he had once been, a presence
even on the battlefield in the Six-Day War, or so family legend had it. At the end of the prayer he kept his eyes closed
and went on to recite very quickly and at length another
Hebrew prayer that nobody else seemed to know. When he

stopped they all sat in silence. Gradually the conversation level rose.

'Poor Miriam,' the woman across from Wolf said to no one in particular. She was the wife of the man directly opposite Wolf. She hadn't once looked at Wolf, nor had she spoken to him or acknowledged his presence in any way. On the table in front of her was a single bottle of wine which was supposed to serve the whole table. Wolf reached for it and filled his glass.

'She had the world at her feet that girl,' the woman said again. 'All the boys at schul were so crazy about her, that's what I always remember. She could have had her pick of any of them!'

She listed names.

'Jonah Horowitz. Ari Raban. Rahm Eisenberg. Not to mention our Noah, who simply adored the ground she walked on.'

Her husband hurried to say something to Wolf about London, asking him what part he lived in. Wolf was momentarily taken aback by the question. It didn't make any sense to him. He'd been living in London for years.

'London. Yes,' he said, a little irritated.

The man waited for him to say more, but Wolf just looked back at him. The man went on to say that he had taken a sabbatical in King's back in the '70s. He seemed like a benign and intelligent old man, a retired cardiologist apparently. He'd known Lenny, Avram's brother, ever since his NYU days.

'Back then it was hard for a Jew to get a medical job in this country,' the man said. 'Certainly in any of the decent places . . . After fellowship I hit a brick wall, so it was a good time to go overseas. I had a good time there in London. We both did. Could have stayed, as a matter of fact. Isn't that right, hon?'

'What? Yes . . . well, here is home,' the woman next to him said, now looking at Wolf, 'among our family and friends, our *people*.' She tapped her finger on the table as she spoke, then looked away and spoke to Judy.

'I didn't realize that,' Wolf said to the man. 'I would have thought the medical profession was one of the fairly open ones. For Jewish people.'

'Not at all,' the doctor replied, and he started to carefully fold his napkin, taking care that the creases were exact. 'There were virtually no Jews at the top of any of the medical professions until the late '60s. Psychiatry perhaps being the sole exception.'

Wolf knocked back more of his wine before filling his glass again. It was kosher, predictably sweet and tasted like it had been left out in the sun. Regardless, it seemed to be doing the trick. He felt more relaxed.

'What do you do yourself?' the doctor asked him.

Again the directness of the question threw Wolf. The big earnest face staring back at him, waiting for him to answer.

'That's a good question,' he said, laughing, taking up more of the wine. Frankly he found the whole thing absurd.

The doctor smiled.

A wicker basket full of yarmulkes was passed around. Some of the men, including the old doctor, were already wearing their own, having taken them out from their jacket pockets when Avram had started the proceedings. Wolf was the only male not wearing one. Some of the younger boys reached into the basket, selecting ones that were multi-coloured and not the usual bland discus. When the basket came to Wolf he passed it on without taking one and he felt the eyes of the room on him, but when he looked up nobody was in fact looking at him except for the woman across from him. She was wearing a small woolen yarmulke, blue and white, the colours of Israel.

Throughout the meal Miriam was referred to continuously. Judy above all spoke about her, recounting several sweet anecdotes from Miriam's childhood. She directed herself towards Ruth, but occasionally she also addressed him. Ruth looked like she wanted to vanish into the ground, but part of her was also eager to hear any mention of her mother. Every so often Judy's eyes became full and tears would shoot perpendicularly down her face, although she was smiling the entire time. Wolf wasn't used to the dead being spoken about like this, so openly, as if they simply hadn't been able to make it. Growing up, his own family's dead were never mentioned at all, neither his grandmothers, whom he had never met, nor his grandfathers, only one of whom he had met and news of whose passing was his first awareness of death. That was his father's father, and he had got to know him a bit. He visited them from Germany on two prolonged occasions, spending two summers in a row in Dublin. The second was a heatwave summer and Wolf had a small number of vivid memories of it. West Germany had won the

World Cup. He had watched the games with his grandfather as his father had no interest. The old man spoke not a word of English, but this had an equalizing effect on their relationship as it removed any authority, and Wolf remembered being aware of this. The other thing he remembered very clearly was that his grandfather's right leg was stiffly straight and wouldn't bend an inch. He had to put it up on the sofa. Wolf's father told him it was a war injury and he asked his grandfather whether he'd been shot, but the old man just said, No, matter-of-factly. Some time after that Wolf came home from school and his father was up in his bedroom with the curtains drawn and the door closed. 'His father is dead,' Wolf's mother said tersely, as if it was something that had happened to Wolf's father as a result of his own ineptitude. Wolf made an attempt at crying because he felt that that was what you were supposed to do, but his mother just looked at him, irritated. He was in her way, she said, she needed to get something out of the cupboard. She knew full well that he didn't feel anything, certainly no real grief – the news was abstract, the old man had been living in a different country, and most of the time it was like he was dead anyway. Wolf couldn't remember what he looked like and his father alone travelled to Germany for the funeral. His grandfather then joined the ranks of their silent dead, the rest of their extended family back in Germany whom Wolf had never met and who were never mentioned, and whose existence was only attested to by black-and-white photographs, thirty or so of them, which lay loose in the bottom drawer of the cabinet in their never-used dining room. Wolf was

very curious about the people in those photographs, especially the young boys around his own age. They seemed to
be his father's family, large groups of smiling fair-haired children and adults among whom he could make out his father
at various identifiable stages of youth, surrounded by friends
or cousins and adults who bore a resemblance to him. There
were a few later photos of his parents also, looking stern and
serious, standing apart on their wedding day, his father in
Buddy Holly glasses, and even a few from their honeymoon
in Switzerland, hiking and presumably having a good time,
even if it wasn't so apparent. His mother's family weren't in
any of the photographs, with the exception of a picture of an
old woman standing alone in a formal portrait-like image,
and a separate image of the same woman standing beside his
mother. 'Mutter, Hannover 1950' was written on the back
of it in pencil.

'I remember your wedding.'

It was the woman next to him. It was the first thing she
had said to him all evening, but she immediately turned
away. A minute later the woman leaned in to him again.

'I went to it for Miriam's sake,' she said. 'Even though the
rebbe told me not to . . . Anyway, it's like it was yesterday. You
wore a blue suit with an enormous white flower. It was the
size of this . . .'

He looked down to see that she had formed her hand into
a fist.

'Miriam . . .' she continued, 'Miriam was . . . well . . . so special, such a beautiful person.' And then she stopped and put

her hands in the air. She looked at him and shook her head. 'Anyway...I remember it,' she said. She turned back to him once more. The suddenness of her movements surprised him. 'Here. Have more wine,' and she refilled his glass in a manner that was almost violent.

'That's fine,' he said, but she kept pouring until the wine was up to the brim and the bottle was empty. The entire table was now looking at Wolf's glass, which was overflowing.

'Does anybody have a straw?' Wolf asked, but nobody laughed and there was an uncomfortable silence around the table. Ruth slumped a little in her seat with her hand over her eyes.

'Which reminds me, Wolfgang,' Allen said then. 'When's Miriam's ceremony? It's on the fifth, right? At the Hudson?'

The whole table was waiting for Wolf to speak, but he had no idea what Allen was on about. He felt that sense of panic rising in his throat, his face flushing. All these people looking at him. Who were they, anyway? What did they want with him? He could feel himself getting angry, he was liable to lash out at them.

'Yes. The fifth,' a voice said. He was surprised to see that it was his daughter Ruth who had spoken. She was sitting at the other end of the table. He had forgotten she was there and was pleased to see her.

'What? You're doing it on Yom Kippur?!' the woman across from Wolf said.

'That's Mum's birthday,' Ruth said. 'Or was anyway.'

'A cremation on Yom Kippur?!' the woman said. 'Avram? You knew about this?!'

'Well, to be fair,' Judy said, 'the cremation already happened. It's just a ceremony by the water. I think it'll be kind of nice actually. We'll all be together. And Miriam requested that it be on her birthday. Maybe she didn't realize it was Yom Kippur.'

'Actually she did,' Ruth said. 'She kind of liked the idea.'

'It is a mitzvah to bury the dead,' the woman with the yarmulke said, and here she pointed her index finger down at the table. 'Our tradition calls it a *chesed shel emet*, a true act of kindness. Burying the dead is a core Jewish value. When Sarah dies in Genesis, Abraham goes to great lengths to acquire an *achuzat kever* for her. I ask you: why did Abraham go to such trouble if it's not important?'

She was now looking straight at Wolf.

'We Jews view our bodies as gifts from God – evidence of God's love for us. In life we are forbidden to harm them, and in death we are commanded to treat them with dignity. This,' and again she pressed down on the table, 'is the way we honour our dead.'

At the head of the table, Avram's stillness, eyes closed, called to mind a sculpture made of sand.

'Cremation,' he said with obvious distaste. He shook his head slowly. Then he opened his eyes and looked around the table. 'You know that after they burn they pound?' he said. 'With iron tool. They pound. They pound the bone to powder ... Pound it. Even the *luz*.'

'Well,' Judy said, 'as opposed to what, Uncle? Lying in the ground and decomposing ... which has personally always freaked me out. Or you could do it like they do in Israel, paying a fortune to get one of those spots in that cemetery on the hill so that when the Messiah comes you roll down it like a zombie.'

Avram shook his head again as if he didn't want to hear any more.

Wolf looked in Avram's direction and waited for some silence around the table. Then he said: 'This is what she wanted. So this is what we will do.'

Now his own index finger was pointing down at the table, and from the prolonged silence that followed and the way in which everyone was looking at him it was clear that his words had been spoken with more firmness and more aggression than he had intended.

13

IT TOOK A while for the computer to start up. At the far
end of the room was a large fish tank. Classical music emanated from the walls. The blank screen eventually ceased its
flickering and stared back at him. He tried to ignore the anxiety he could feel building inside him. Anything remotely
mechanical or technical seemed to bring it on. He took some
deep breaths. A man in a suit walked into the room and
stood behind Wolf.

'You found the office then?' the man said.

Wolf turned to him. The man's badge said the words Exec.
Manager and beneath that his name.

He came closer to him and picked up a cup of old coffee
that Wolf now noticed.

'So how is the old man?'

Wolf didn't say anything and the Exec. Manager laughed.

'I thought so,' he said. 'Anyway, let me know if you need
any assistance. I told Avram I'd take care of you and your
daughter during your stay here. Him and my old man go
back a long way, practically to the boat.'

He turned and left and now there was no one else in the
room. The computer came to life and Wolf hit a few of the
keys. To his relief he found it relatively easy to get onto his

email. He didn't even need to consult his notebook for his login information. In recent months he'd entered everything in the back pages, all his passwords, codes, you name it.

There were several emails from the London property management company. He didn't respond to any of their queries. Maurice would handle all of that. A URL was embedded in one of the emails, linking to the web page that showed the listing. He clicked on it, and saw that their house was up on the website already. They had done a good job of staging the photographs, making it look brand new, as if no one had ever lived there. All of their things had been removed and placed in storage. He took the virtual tour, barely recognizing the rooms, the perspectives different from how his memory saw them – everything appeared smaller, cramped, the main bedroom bare, the bed having been removed, the built-in wardrobes relics from the '70s which Miriam always talked of changing but never got around to, the full-length mirror on the inside of one of the doors capturing her image every day for twenty years only to forget it just as quickly each time. The house could have belonged to anyone, the carpet was picked clean, there was no trace of them any more or the years they'd spent living there. A separate firm was responsible for that, cleaning the building to the bone. They were like magic, they come to your home and pack up everything, even bits of paper and rubbish off the floor, you don't have to lift a finger. Afterwards there is no trace of you, as if you had never existed in the first place.

As far as Ruth was concerned, everything was just as they had left it, waiting for them to return. He had arranged for the movers to come the day they left for New York, after they had departed for the airport. His own things were to be destroyed, but all of Ruth's belongings were to be shipped to her in a couple of months, once she had settled in New York, even the contents of her bedroom wastepaper basket – he didn't dare throw anything out – along with certain memorabilia belonging to Miriam, her sketch pad, various framed photographs, jewellery, items of clothing which he thought Ruth might want, might even wear at some stage, make-up, other trinkets and ornaments. The majority of Miriam's clothes he decided in the end to give away. The company arranged this. There was also Miriam's collection of textbooks, which he thought long and hard about donating. Really he should have done that, it was the logical thing, and Miriam would have wanted him to do it, but out of all her things he found this impossible. He put them into storage. There were so many of these books, a testament to Miriam's never-ending career as a mature student, which began when they first moved to London when she enrolled in the Open University, studying science, a subject which had intim-idated her as an adolescent. In time she got her A levels, before going on to qualify as a secondary school teacher in biology, but she didn't stop there, piling on additional degrees and two master's. Perhaps one of the main regrets about her illness was that she could not now achieve the doctorate she badly wanted. The textbooks used to be stacked in thick piles in the spare room, more than a hundred of them, arranged around a desk she never once used, as she preferred to study in the kitchen, at night by the window, which, on account of the angle of the house, faced outward towards no man-made structure and was a plane of the purest black.

14

HE WANTED TO show her the subway. This seemed like something he should do. It was a small thing, but it was eminently practical and something he thought he could manage. There was even the foolish thought that perhaps every time she took the subway in the future she might remember him. He had written it down on each of his daily itineraries. Show R the subway system. It came as a disappointment to see that she clearly already knew where to go, how to negotiate the system, and he ended up mostly following her as she led him through the turnstiles for Uptown, despite the fact that she didn't know where they were headed specifically. Where they were going was a surprise. A surprise, she had said. What am I, twelve?

They got off the 6 at Lexington Avenue, then walked crosstown to the Plaza Hotel. Midtown was its usual chaotic self. The sun was getting up to full tilt. Some of the businessmen had their jackets hooked over their shoulders, their white shirts glaring. The melting asphalt. The pungent pretzel stands. Tourists carrying maps, dressed as if they were on safari. Wolf took off his jacket and carried it. Ruth was in her usual all-black. As they passed a vagrant sitting on a strip of cardboard, Wolf fished in his pocket before continuing on.

'Did you just give that man twenty dollars?'

'So?'

She was staring at him in disbelief.

'You're supposed to give it to charity instead.'

'I don't know. Seems like hard work to me. Just sitting there all day. They must be bored out of their skulls.'

'It enables their habits, Mike, is the reason.'

'Well, if it allows them to escape their misery for a few hours I don't have a problem with it.'

Ruth shook her head then picked up her pace so that she was a few steps ahead of him. When they got to the Apple store on Fifth Avenue they saw the tour bus in the distance, emblazoned on its side with pictures of the women from the TV show *Sex and the City*. Ruth realized what the surprise was.

'Are you serious?'

'I thought you liked this show? Your mother did.'

Ruth looked miserable.

'It was mine and Mum's thing.'

He thought she was going to start crying.

'We don't have to do it. I thought it would be a fun way to show you the city.'

'Like I've told you a hundred times, Mike, I already know the city.'

They crossed the road and waited in the queue outside the bus, which was parked directly in front of the Plaza Hotel. Ruth was silent the entire time. Shortly after eleven the doors of the bus opened and they got on. It was only a quarter full, if even that. It was all women, apart from two men sitting separately on their own. Everybody was calm and quiet, looking out at Fifth Avenue and the packed sidewalks. Most of the people on the tour didn't seem like tourists – one of the men was wearing a tie and eating a sandwich, and looked like he was on his lunch break. The exception was a group of four middle-aged women sitting near the back, each of them wearing sweaters patterned with the Stars and Stripes. After a while the tour guide boarded the bus, a small dark-haired woman in a flashy gold top. She introduced herself as Courtney, and walked down the aisle with a microphone headset attached to the side of her face.

'So are y'all ready to have some sex?' she shouted. The microphone gave off high-pitched feedback, causing everyone to grimace. She repeated the question, and the only response was from the four women in the Stars and Stripes jumpers. Yeah. You betcha. Each of them was carrying a small bottle of soft drink, and the two in front said, Cheers and tapped their bottles off each other and drank from them.

'Well I'm gonna be your sexpert today!' the guide continued. 'And I can explain why at the end over a cosmo!'

The Stars and Stripes women cheered. Woohoo!

'So we've just left the Plaza,' the guide continued, 'where, of course, Mr Big marries Natasha.'

As she spoke, multiple on-board video screens appeared and the show's recognizable soundtrack from the opening credits sounded loudly. Everyone cheered. Ruth turned away and looked out the window, and Wolf pretended to do the same, but really he was looking at his daughter, studying her. She had his own mother's high cheekbones, her most striking feature, like a high-born Aryan. Sensing him, Ruth turned around and he pretended to be looking beyond her out the window, resting his eyes on the crowds going up and down the sidewalk, the endless activity which he could watch for hours without getting bored, it was similar to when you look out at an ocean.

'I never got what your mother liked about this show.'

'What's not to get?'

'I suppose there's the whole New York thing. Presumably she just liked seeing all the familiar places.'

'There's no great big mystery to it, you know. You don't have to overanalyze it.'

The bus turned left and went onto Madison and then drove uptown and around the Upper East Side, passing something which Courtney the guide called the Friar Fuck church. Every now and again she pointed out the odd house or building where some transient character in the show had supposedly lived or where a party or event took place which the protagonists had gone to. To his surprise, much of what she referred to was familiar to him. He must have absorbed more than he realized of the show, which played constantly in their house. It was Miriam's guilty pleasure, particularly over the past year, when she was in no position to travel to New York in person.

As they were driving through Times Square he noticed a billboard advertising a Broadway show. A group of people were on the billboard, one woman and a few men, all dressed up in costume. The woman reminded him of someone. Down a block or two they passed the same billboard, a smaller version of it, and this time he paid more attention to it, turning to look back at it.

'What's the matter, Mike? Spot some talent back there, did you?'

'I thought I recognized someone. On one of the bill-boards. A friend,' he said, which sounded disingenuous even to his own ears. Ruth gave an almost imperceptible shake of her head and looked down at the sidewalk. She then shifted position, putting her knees up against the back of the seat in front of her, and sat back, closing her eyes. The Stars and Stripes women were the only ones on the bus doing any talking. The bus got mired in traffic and was barely moving. Ruth's breathing was regular, and it was clear she was sleeping. Even the Stars and Stripes women were silent now, looking out the window, and the air was warm and heavy.

They got off the bus downtown in the Village along with everyone else. There was a sex shop right there and they all marched into it. The shop was cramped and cheap-looking and empty. The man behind the counter was a skinhead, heavily tattooed, but when he spoke he seemed benevolent, almost childlike, smiling and chatting away to Courtney the tour guide, whom he clearly knew from previous trips. Wolf and Ruth remained standing by the door. A customer came through it and Ruth moved awkwardly to get herself out of his way, almost bumping into the man. She stood up against the window, folding and unfolding her arms a few times, clearly very uncomfortable. It was as if she didn't know where to look or how to hold herself. In the window display was an inflatable doll dressed all in leather, its rear end open to the elements, a very visible arsehole, coloured black. Wolf pointed it out to Ruth.

'Gross,' she said.

He stood in front of her. Ruth didn't know where to look.

'Have you ever . . .'

'Jesus Christ!' said Ruth. There was a look of pure panic on her face and she made a lurch towards the door.

He reached over and opened it for her and she practically burst through it as if in need of oxygen. He followed her.

'I was only going to ask if you had been in this sort of place before.'

Ruth took a deep breath, regaining her composure a little.

'These places are for your generation, Mike. It's quite tragic really.'

She gave him a forced smile, then leaned back against the wall. She took out her phone and focused on it, raising her foot behind her and planting it on the wall. He remained in front of her, facing her, observing her, but this time not looking for any residue of his wife. Instead, he looked at Ruth as she was, how she was dressed, which really was quite conservative, at least according to what appeared to be the norm for teenage girls these days. Jeans that were too big for her, a bad fit by the looks of things, heavy Doc boots that were clearly well worn, the laces frayed, and that must surely be uncomfortable in this heat. A T-shirt with a large star on it.

'What's Chabad House?' he asked, reading what was on her T-shirt. 'Is it some metal band?'

She ignored him. He was still studying her T-shirt, the image on it which he couldn't make sense of.

'And the star,' he said. 'Christ, you're not a Scientologist, are you?'

She finally looked up at him.

'It's the Star of David, Mike. But no, I don't suppose you'd recognize it.'

She went back to her phone, but he kept looking at her. She must have been really absorbed in her phone because she didn't notice him looking at her. He wondered if she was still a virgin.

'It must be difficult for your generation,' he said.

She was doing her best to ignore him.

'Ruth?'

Finally she looked up at him. What was he on about now?

'I mean, to grow up in this era,' he said, 'with all the pressures that you guys have to put up with. The social media and all that.'

'The social media?' she said.

'Not to mention the rest of it,' he said. 'You know, internet porn and all.'

Her face as she looked back at him was pure disbelief.

'What are you on about, you perv?'

'No, no, I'm being serious,' he said. 'It's a really serious issue. It's one of the things I worry about.'

'Yeah, well, I expect you'd know all about it, wouldn't you.'

He went to say something else but stopped. He really

did worry for Ruth and her generation of men, the ones she would have to placate, how the internet was wiring their brains for them.

A young girl walked by, probably not that much older than Ruth. They both looked at her, she was practically half naked.

'What do you think of her?'

Ruth looked at him, again with disbelief.

'Do you think she's attractive?'

She was still just staring at him.

'I meant for you!' he said. 'I just wondered was she your type at all?'

Ruth didn't seem to know where to begin.

'Are you on drugs?' she said.

She shook her head, then returned to her phone. He left her in peace and went back to his spot on the other side of the door.

When the rest of the tour came out of the shop, Courtney the guide gathered them together before leading them on a walk through the West Village. With the microphone clipped to her chin, she pointed out many landmarks from the show, places where certain scenes had occurred, and shops or restaurants which had featured.

Ruth looked around her as they walked and seemed at least somewhat interested.

'Can you see your mother doing this tour?' he asked her.

'Are you insane?'

Wolf laughed. He watched her closely as they strolled

along. He liked the idea of Ruth being a New Yorker. Just like he had always liked the idea of Miriam being one. It was after all the centre of the world, a form of privilege. She'd fit in well here. It would be good for her. London brought out the sarkiness in her, which admittedly she was good at, but America would be a healthy change. They didn't speak a single word the entire way. He noticed one or two faces turning to look at her, she seemed taller, pale, her hair long and full, that reddish tint to it clearly visible. He was proud to be walking alongside her.

Many photographs were taken on the steps where the main character played by Sarah Jessica Parker had lived. There was a sign on the railing saying Quiet Please, Real People Live Here. He asked Ruth if she wanted her photo taken and was surprised when she said OK and stood over by the lower step looking at the ground. But then just before he took it she said, Wait, and she went to stand beside the sign stating that real people lived there.

'Take me next to this,' she said.

The next stop was the Magnolia Bakery, where they queued for cupcakes. The line went out of the shop and all the way around the corner, but it was pleasant standing in the leafy shade. A warm breeze came to them from the west side. It had a taint of the ocean, which it was easy to forget wasn't far away, only a few blocks. The queue moved quickly and Ruth ordered cupcakes, taking the money from him when he was too slow to give it to the woman. He went across the street to the Starbucks but lost his concentration in the queue and became panicked, forgetting what he had gone in for. He came back empty-handed.

'Perhaps you'd go in?' he said to her. 'It's a bit of a melee in there. I'm feeling a bit light-headed.'

Reluctantly she took his wallet off him, and she returned a few minutes later with a chai latte for herself and for him an enormous black coffee. They sat outside until they saw the rest of the tour come out of Magnolia's, then walked the couple of blocks back to the bus.

'Mum would have liked this part,' he said.

Ruth was silent. She looked away. He couldn't see her face but knew that it was pure pain. As she walked a few paces ahead of him she used the sleeve of her T-shirt to wipe at her eyes. He wanted to put his arm around her but couldn't bring himself to do it in a manner which would appear natural and effortless.

The last stop was in Chelsea at a restaurant.

'You'll recognize this place from the first movie's rehearsal dinner scene,' Courtney told them as the bus stopped, pulling up alongside the parked cars and simply coming to a halt, causing drivers behind them to hammer on their horns angrily. As she spoke a man came out of the restaurant and opened the door. He waved at Courtney and she waved back while still talking to them.

'There's Eddie, right on cue,' she said, waving to him. 'Now, ladies, watch yourselves. He's got roving hands, does fast Eddie...I don't know, maybe you want some attention after all this sex talk!'

The Stars and Stripes women hooted, one of them gagged on the bottle she had held up to her mouth, causing the others to laugh even more.

They got off the bus and were directed into the restaurant. The man greeted Courtney and handed them small set menus printed on postcard-sized paper, with the heading 'Sex and the City Brunch'.

'OK, people,' Courtney shouted out, breaking off from the man. 'Obviously there's brunch available if you're not stuffed with cupcakes. But really this is where we drink!'

As she shouted she put her arms around a big cardboard cut-out of the show and pointed to lettering signifying discounted cosmopolitans. The Stars and Stripes women cheered. The whole tour moved away from the entrance and towards the enormous bar. The owner of the restaurant started pouring pre-made cocktails from a jug. Wolf got one and also ordered a Scotch. He held out the cocktail to Ruth.

'Are you serious?' she said.

'What's the matter?'

'Eh, the fact that I'm sixteen maybe!'

'Come on, let's have a drink together,' he said. 'It won't kill you.'

She stared at him in disbelief before finally accepting the glass from him and then holding it awkwardly. He looked around at the crowd which surrounded them. Out of the corner of his eye he saw Ruth take up the cocktail and drink some of it. The bartender gave him his drink and he turned back to face Ruth. She smiled, already more relaxed, as if the alcohol had had an immediate effect. One of the Stars and Stripes women turned and started talking to him.

'Liquor just makes everything better, don't it?' she said.

'Are they any good?' he asked, nodding at the cocktail she had in her hand.

'Oh, anything's good at this stage. But we've been sloshing our way around the whole tour. I mean, really, how could you do it otherwise?'

He must have looked confused because the woman lifted the small bottle of Coca-Cola she was carrying and said, 'Ole J.D. here never lets me down.' Then she pointed at the bottles the other women were holding.

'Vodka, vodka, gin,' she said for each of them in turn.

They all laughed. It was their first time in New York. They had met at a support group in Houston called Mothers of Fallen Heroes. When he heard this Wolf reached out his own drink and the woman tapped her bottle off it.

'To our fallen heroes,' he said, surprised to find no trace of irony in his voice.

'Amen,' she replied, and they repeated the act of tipping their drinks against each other. Even Ruth got in on the action. They stood beside each other in silence, listening to the din of the others all around them. The woman turned to him and asked him did he know any good steak houses in the city that didn't cost an arm and a leg?

15

HE HAD NO idea where Ruth was. Two cups of coffee stood on the low table in front of him which he had no memory of ordering. Plus there was milk in one of them. How Miriam drank such milky coffee was beyond him, as well as the fact that it could sit for hours until it was stone cold, and that wouldn't bother her either. He leaned over and put his little finger in it. Yes, cold. She'd probably come any minute now and drink it all up, even enjoy it. He looked around him. It seemed he was in the lobby of a hotel, over in the corner on the large couch by the window. The material of the blinds cast an intricate map of light all around him. He sat in it, blinded, but it was not unpleasant. The lobby was neither busy nor quiet. There was frequent traffic through it, which he found calming. Every time he looked over at the reception desk there was someone else standing there behind it. A young man there now, who made eye contact with him. The man stepped out from behind the desk and started to come his way until he was standing right in front of Wolf.

'More coffee for you guys?' he said.

'No thanks.'

'You found the bank OK?'

'Yes,' Wolf said, aware that he was being a little abrupt.

But still the man stood there. His badge said the words Exec. Manager and beneath that his name.

'You know, when I was young I used to call him Uncle Avram,' the man said. 'He and my father were very close back then. We used to go to their house for the holidays. I remember Miriam. She was a good bit older than me, but still . . .'

The man's voice tailed off. Wolf just looked at him.

'Anyway,' the man said, before stooping to pick up one of the coffee cups but leaving the other one, then heading back to his desk. Wolf closed his eyes. The sun was making him drowsy. He could easily nod off. What the hell was keeping Miriam anyway? They were due to go somewhere, although he wasn't sure where exactly. Perhaps that memorial in the forest she was always on about. They would have to rent a car, perhaps they could get one at the airport. But how would they get out there? A woman came out of the lift and walked towards him. An attractive younger woman in a black dress, dark hair, a reddish tint to it. He was surprised when the woman walked towards him. She came right over to where he was sitting and picked up the remaining coffee cup and drank from it.

'Shall we get going then?' she said. 'We're going to be late.'

16

THEY GOT OFF the 1 train at 96th Street and climbed up the narrow steps, emerging onto Broadway. He stood for a second to get his bearings, where uptown, downtown were, although Ruth seemed to know this instinctively and was already standing over by the pedestrian walkway waiting for the light to change, looking back at him with impatience. They crossed the avenue and headed westward downhill in the direction of the river.

'Your mother used to live around here.'

From the almost reverent look Ruth gave him it was clear she didn't know this. Any evidence of Miriam's New York life prior to their London existence fascinated Ruth. Or more specifically that part of her New York life before she had met him, when she was free and single and only a girl herself, not much older than Ruth was now.

'Back the other way a block,' he said.

'Where exactly? Who did she live with?'

'It was just off Amsterdam Avenue ... I'm pretty sure 94th Street, with five other girls.'

Ruth stared at him and he knew she would hang on his every word, so he took his time. His mind was as clear as if there was a breeze running through it. It was like that every now and again, moments where he could recall everything, all at once, with almost perfect clarity.

'That was when I met her first,' he said. 'It was a three-bed...but they bought these dividers in IKEA and turned it into a six-bed...It was very chaotic. Really untidy, the sink was always full of dirty dishes and the living room was dark and cramped. Made her cello practising virtually impossible.'

'Who did she live with?'

'Nobody you'd know...Nobody she kept in contact with. It was all people she'd met at her summer camp if I remember rightly. All Jewish. One of them was a freelance journalist, a real right-winger, at least when it came to the Palestinians. I remember she had this thing about not flushing the toilet, to save water...I think she was the one who created most of the mess in the apartment – she rarely left it, was always on her computer...She moved to Israel eventually I think. Probably to one of those settlements.'

'Just because you're pro-Israel doesn't mean you're right wing,' Ruth said. 'Just like not *all* the Germans were Nazis.'

'She was a Ruth also I think.'

They passed a basketball court; a game was taking place. Both of them slowed and looked at it for a minute.

'I don't know,' Wolf said. 'Anyone's capable of anything if you ask me. In the right environment.'

It was as if Ruth didn't hear him. They continued walking.

'Anyway. She lived back there,' he said. 'When she was at Juilliard. I'll show you later if you'd like. Specifically.'

Ruth looked at him. She was on the verge of tears.

They continued down in the direction of Riverside Park

79

and the water. As they descended the fairly steep incline they began to see more of the river, the Henry Hudson Parkway held up over it on pillars, the cars zipping along on it like the toy cars he used to play with as a child. Even their noise seemed muted in the thick late-summer air. It was now another beautiful early evening, the light beginning to fade a touch, but leaving a gorgeous blue tinge to everything. The heavy clouds of earlier had moved on. The Hudson was silver backed, the New Jersey Palisades and the buildings on the far side of the river covered in heat mist. When they got close to their destination they saw a crowd of people by the water, and even from here, as they waited to cross Riverside Drive, he could see that a lot of the men in the crowd were wearing skullcaps. He also now saw the rest of the family – Avram, Judy, Allen and some of their children – standing on the other side of the road waiting for them.

The ceremony they were headed to was called Tashlich. Growing up, it had been Miriam's favourite of the many rituals she had had to endure. She wanted him to bring Ruth to it, certainly this year, but also every year if possible. It was important to her, one of the few rituals she considered important. Tashlich. He said the word out loud to himself, its satisfying harshness.

'It's the most spiritual of the organized things they do,' Miriam had said to him. 'It's held outdoors and not confined or stuffy, listening endlessly to some boring rabbi drone on and on.'

They were in the living room of their house in Islington

having this conversation. It was only about two months before Miriam died, and that afternoon they had had some good news. Or rather what passed for good news during those last ten months. Less growth in the tumour than had been expected.

'Within the realm of stability,' the consultant had told them in the clinic that afternoon.

He was wearing a suit and was surrounded by other more junior doctors in white coats. Wolf had got to know the consultant's little entourage a bit, and this time they were all visibly more relaxed in their faces and manner, and this was good enough for him. He insisted on buying champagne on the way home, but it stayed in the fridge. Miriam said she was exhausted and wanted to just vegetate on the couch. Later on that night she planned to watch *Sex and the City*, the new movie. She said she wanted to see a bit of New York. Ruth was upstairs on the desktop in the study downloading it for her from iTunes. She was going to watch it also. He was just leaving the living room when out of the blue Miriam said:

'There's one additional thing I want you to be sure to do,' and she patted the space beside her. 'Come here.' And he went over and sat beside her like a little boy.

She told him about the Tashlich ceremony, which he'd attended once with her twenty years previously when they both lived in New York. Miriam seemed to have forgotten this, but he remembered it clearly, standing with all the Jews of the Upper West Side as they gathered by the Hudson on what he remembered to have been a cool evening. There were prayers, and then people took out loaves of bread and broke them into pieces, putting the bread on the surface of the water to symbolize the cleansing of what Christians would call sin. For the Jews it is more a question of clearing the decks. You will ask for forgiveness and repent. You will atone. God will, hopefully, write you into the Book of Life and then he will seal it. The slate will be wiped clean, congratulations, you get one more year, do better. He liked the tradition. It seemed a lot more forgiving than the Christian way, where you have to wait until the very end of things before you pitch up in front of Peter at the pearly gates, only to find that it is miles too late, that you're already totally screwed because of everything you have done or not done in your life, an infinite number of things, it makes you feel faint just thinking about it, beginning as a small child when even then you knew better, you always knew better.

'It's spiritual,' Miriam said. 'To be in amongst a big group of you standing there. I don't know … it's not just a Jewish thing … it's more a human thing … that you look around and … you're throwing your bits of bread or paper into the water … and you just feel, I don't know … that you're all in the same boat I guess.'

She looked at him, unsure as to whether she had adequately explained it to him.

'Plus there's something about the physical act of casting your "faults" onto the water. It sounds ridiculous but it's like you're seeing how identical your flaws are to everyone else's, how identical you are to everyone else,' she said. 'It's funny, but you actually do feel better afterwards.' She paused and looked off towards infinity, before continuing, 'I suppose we're simple primitive creatures when all is said and done.'

She wanted Ruth to go.

'Even if it's the only Jewish thing she does. I don't care about the rest of it. Or most of the rest of it. But that I think is one of the important things.'

He gave her his word and she laughed at how serious he had suddenly become, 'like a knight'.

He picked up the tray of food she had left untouched and stood up to leave, in a bit of a rush. He didn't really want to be having this type of conversation, where death was a consideration, even a participant in it, like another person whose wishes had to be factored in. They had just had good news, for Christ's sake. Now was the time not to think about things, but rather to go back to normal life where, for a brief lull, you can carry on as if for forever and forget about those things, just like everybody else does, everybody else in the world, that is, apart from you, or so it certainly seems as you see them all strolling idly by or in a rush for work or laughing or standing in line or in small chatty groups or driving along while singing to music – you can see them clearly through the windscreen, their mouths moving, but they don't see you behind your own invisible pane of glass through which you seem to be viewing everything, like a diver lowered into the depths, into a world that is not real, no matter that it is right there in front of your eyes.

'We don't need to discuss this now,' he said to Miriam, sharper than he had intended, although she didn't seem to notice what he was saying. She was staring into the distance, lost in thought.

'Watch your chick flick,' he said then, a bit softer.

But Miriam was in that other mood.

'Whatever God is you're more likely to feel it with the wind on your face, don't you think?' she said to him. He looked at her and saw in her expression the uncertainty which he used to project onto her all the time, expecting to have it explained to him, and to be reassured. He wasn't used to seeing it in Miriam's face, fear and doubt laid bare, and it terrified him. He put down the tray and went back over to her and they embraced and both of them cried and didn't say anything else.

For now we are OK, he remembered thinking as he hugged his wife. Right here, right now. We are safe at this particular moment.

They heard Ruth's footsteps on the stairs, coming down. They quickly wiped their eyes and he stood up and took the tray out to the kitchen.

'Wolfgang, I know what to buy you for your birthday,' Avram shouted as Ruth and he crossed the road and approached the old man and the rest of the family. 'A watch which I will set for you fifteen minutes early.'

As he walked towards them, Wolf was struck by how vigorous his father-in-law appeared, just as in Allen and Judy's house he had been struck in the opposite way by how close to death the old man had seemed. Avram bounced up and down on his feet and then rushed to Ruth, gathering her into his embrace, even lifting her in the air a few inches. He was wearing a light blue shirt and navy pants, no doubt clothes which Judy had bought him.

'My child,' he said to Ruth after embracing her. 'Come,' he said, 'let's get a place near to the water.'

Allen was also standing off to the side with the three youngest of his four children. Ruth broke off from her grandfather and stood on her own, near her cousins but separate from them. Wolf noticed again that awkwardness in her body language. He could only guess as to whether it was shyness or if she disliked them. Probably a mixture of both. They were good kids, a little indulged perhaps, soft and naïve, but that's probably what she needed now, to be around people like that. Ruth had had a tough time of things back in London, especially during the years he wasn't around. He didn't know many of the details, but Miriam had had to take her out of one school. A 'bad patch' was all she'd told him. Ruth seemed mostly fine in her current school, to him at any rate, which perhaps didn't mean much. Although there had been one unpleasant incident that he was aware of, anti-Semitism essentially, when it was found out that she attended Hebrew school. It didn't help that the sole other individual from her school who also went was a bit of an oddball. It was no huge deal, things written on her desk or locker, practical jokes which seemed to have an edge to them. Ruth herself seemed to take it mostly in her stride.

They found a place near the water on the periphery of the crowd. There must have been a few hundred people there already, spread along the Hudson's edge, maybe ten deep. They went where the crowd was beginning to thin out a little.

85

'Closer. Closer,' Avram kept turning and saying to them. Allen complained quietly to Judy.

'This is fine, Uncle,' she said, and Avram relented, unhappily, like a little boy.

At the heart of the crowd was a group of rabbis, but not everyone was facing towards them. The crowd was quite mixed and he noticed that some of the people were doing their own thing, saying their own prayers. There were several groups of Orthodox Jews interspersed in pockets among the crowd – Ortho's, as Miriam called them, and for whom she always had a bit of a soft spot. She found them amusing, even fascinating, with their strict adherence to the Torah, their religious supernaturalism. Her best friend growing up had been one. Their lives had separated quite a bit by the time they became teenagers, but they had kept in semi-regular contact. Wolf met the friend once or twice and she was nice enough, a little boring. Her husband sold commercial real estate, but he didn't seem to be very good at it. They got money from her father to buy their place in an Ortho community in Kew Gardens Hills in Queens. Miriam and she grew apart. The whole time Miriam was living in London they spoke on the phone just once, when the friend rang out of the blue to ask her to pray for somebody in her community who was sick. Miriam was happy to hear from her. They spoke for a while, catching up on things, her friend had five children now, but Miriam told him afterwards that the whole time they were speaking it was clear that there was a serious and central purpose behind the phone call. The friend was in earnest when she said that if there was an international dimension to the praying it might make more of an impact. Miriam was bemused, fascinated by it. Obviously he thought it was pathetic, infantile, this sort of religiosity which he took more and more as an affront to the world as it existed in front of his eyes, the sublime and complex, most of which was not even remotely penetrated by the human mind. Why do you need to go and invent cartoon characters and myths, or worse, rely on the ones that were invented two thousand years ago, a time when there were pretty good grounds for your fears as you stared up at a blackening sky whose thunder might as well represent the voice of God, or whose sun might very well decide not to come back tomorrow if you didn't sacrifice to it, a sheep or an ox or your first born? Unless of course it is simply in order to view the same mystery he looked out on as metaphor, which would be OK if it were not for the fact that people take this stuff literally, they really believe this shit – some of them are even prepared to die for it, and to kill. It also pissed him off that Miriam's Ortho friend had to get special dispensation from her rabbi to attend his and Miriam's wedding party, because of his gentile status. They had put effort and money into ensuring they had properly kosher food, but even so the friend didn't eat any of it, and she left before the end. Miriam said she was just happy that she had come.

The majority of the crowd seemed pretty secular. Most people were dressed in regular clothes, some of them very casually. One man was on rollerblades. He threw some bread into the water, then looked up at the sky with his eyes closed and his hands on his hips. After a minute or so he headed off, weaving in and out of the crowd at surprising speed, having to go over the grass a little to get onto the cycle path to head back towards Midtown and Lower Manhattan.

The main rabbi was a dark-haired man in his fifties. Wolf could tell that he was a charismatic man. His voice was powerful, and some of his words reached them on the light water breeze that came down Manhattan's west edge towards them, and that was pleasant and warm on their faces.

'On this Day of Judgement,' he shouted, 'we take account of our lives and relationships during the last year. Of some things we can be proud, of others we must be disappointed or ashamed. We resolve to strengthen and sustain the many mitzvahs we have it in our strength to perform – love in relationships, honesty in business, the repair of the world. And we resolve to cast off the blemishes – those actions or words that we regret. Help us to preserve the good and to cast off the bad. Judge us for life in a year of goodness and blessing.'

Wolf noticed Avram swaying slightly as he listened to the rabbi with his eyes closed. From behind he stared at the back of his father-in-law's skull. The old man's head was much smaller from that angle. Wolf felt that if he stretched out his hand he would be able to hold his entire skull in the palm of his hand, and in his grip everything would be contained, his experiences since childhood, his disappointments, his fears, the history of his entire existence, the triumphs which were so pointless at the end of the day, everything that constitutes a person, how easily it could be crushed.

The rabbi spoke for a while in Hebrew and Wolf's attention passed away from whatever he was saying and out instead to the surroundings – the essentially cloudless sky above them, darkening but still light, the broad grey Hudson with barely any current in it, a vast longitudinal plane of pure silver running through it, the New Jersey Palisades across the way reminding them of ancient things. He became aware of a vast silence, and when he looked around everyone in the crowd was bent over looking at the ground. Ruth muttered urgently to him, telling him to get down. He did so, crouching beside her with his eyes closed. The silence lasted for a long time. He wished that the whole ceremony could be like this. It was a powerful feeling to be in a silent crowd outdoors by the water. It felt like an ancient human thing, the barely audible rabbi, most of his words wrapped up by the air, like an Old Testament Ezekiel or Jacob. All you could hear was the zip of cars on the highway behind them. He felt an affection towards even them, as if he knew something they had yet to find out, with their tiny motor sounds, their sense of hurry to wherever, their futile and comical deadlines and irrelevant money-centred pressures, heading to join those already crowding the buildings of Manhattan behind them, which seemed like alien structures, ridiculous, unnecessary things really, like the set of a big-budget movie.

The episode of silence passed and the rabbi repeated his earlier greeting and explanation of why they had all gathered here for 'the benefit of those at the back who came late'.

A murmur of laughter spread through the crowd.

'We are gathered here on the second day of Rosh Hashanah ... to cleanse ourselves of our sins and to make a promise to the Almighty and to undertake improvements, to try harder even if in reality it is only to fail harder, to fail better.'

Wolf tapped Ruth on the arm. 'I think he just quoted Beckett.'

Ruth shook her head in irritation.

'Quiet!' Avram said, turning to look at him.

Then, taking a yarmulke out of his back pocket, Avram said: 'You must wear this, Wolfgang!'

Wolf took the yarmulke off him and held it in his hand, then put it in his pocket. Ruth noticed and shook her head again but didn't say anything.

The rabbi started singing in Hebrew and his voice rang out very powerfully. Ruth seemed to know the words and spoke them fluently. The prayer changed to English and – chanting it – people turned to face the water. Each of them had in their hands bread, which they broke pieces off and dropped or sprinkled onto the water. Wolf noticed that instead of bread, some people had pieces of paper, which they also rolled up and put onto the water. Behind him was one lady bent over, using her knee as she wrote on some paper in quick handwriting. After a few minutes she stood up and, crumpling the paper, threw it also onto the water. He felt something touch his arm.

'Here,' Ruth said, handing him a roll of bread. Behind her Judy was reaching into a plastic bag and handing out lumps of bread to her kids.

'I made sure it was a big piece,' Ruth added, both smiling and stopping herself from smiling at the same time.

He took the bread and walked to the edge of the water. He broke the bread and crushed it into smaller pieces, and he frittered them between his fingers and onto the water, which was covered with the debris of all the sins of the multitude, cast off and floating on the surface.

17

IT WAS A struggle to make it back up the steep incline that lay in the direction of Broadway. Ruth had marched ahead, stopping every now and again to look back at him with barely concealed impatience. He felt every bit the old man she was seeing before her eyes. Eventually the sidewalk flattened and they stood waiting for the traffic to stop. He tried to get his breath back. The avenue was in its loudest, fullest state, as if all humanity was trying to get someplace else but had to pass through this junction first. Manhattan's iconic steam emanated silently out of the ground beside them. The smell of sewage thickened the air, weighing everything down, suffocating the oxygen. When the pedestrian lights changed they crossed in front of a panting army of yellow cabs, their lights wide-eyed and staring brightly, menacing them in the half-light. Overhead, the buildings crowded over them, leaning in, elbowing each other out of the way to get a good look at them, pressuring the sky, every window in every building lit up. They eventually reached the subway entrance, which stood on a narrow island in the middle of the avenue. Wolf leaned on the metal barrier, still slightly out of breath, before stepping over into the entrance and going down the steps into the cool underground relief.

'Where are you going?' Ruth said.

He stopped and turned around to look up at her. She had remained on the top step of the subway entrance, framed by a rectangle of sky.

'You said you'd show me where Mum lived,' she said.

Her face was slightly panicked, desperate. She was looking directly at him.

'Lived where?' he said.

'What is wrong with you?'

He looked at her. He wasn't trying to be difficult.

'Back there?' she said.

He walked up the steps to her, still at a complete loss.

'You said it was back up there a block. On 94th Street. Where Mum lived with that other Ruth.' She sighed. 'The so-called right-winger.'

'Let's go then,' he said.

They crossed the remainder of the avenue, just making the light before it changed again, then down Broadway a block before heading eastward along 94th Street, which felt right to him, guided more by instinct than memory. He was quiet as they walked, looking up at the buildings, trying to recognize a familiarity in the shapes of the windows, the colour of the walls of the houses, mostly brownstones, some pattern in the fabric of the brick that he might recall. None of it was especially familiar in that all of it was familiar to him, the vaguely shabby Upper West Side where at one point in his life, in those first few months after meeting Miriam, he had spent a lot of time. His life got decided then, dictating everything that was to come afterwards, right up to and including this moment as he walked around accompanied by his daughter.

'This is it,' he said to Ruth, after walking for a while. He almost shouted it out, giddy with relief. It was mostly down to coincidence of course, but still. He stood with his hands on his hips. They were near the far end of the block. He walked over and stood in front of a building with a red door.

'Yes, this is it,' he said again, but more to himself. He looked at Ruth, expecting her to be impressed, but she just stood looking up at the building.

'I don't remember the number,' he said, 'but I remember the way the building dropped a half storey below the ones on either side of it. I always thought that was strange.' Again he had that terrific feeling of clarity. Right now, he could remember just about anything. He took a few steps forward towards the front door. It had barely changed, if at all. The strange and ridiculous thought came to him that if he pressed the right buzzer Miriam would come down the steps and greet them.

'I remember very well standing here waiting for your mother to buzz me in. Mostly she would come down and we would meet halfway on the stairs.'

It was extraordinary. The past seemed to have surrounded him in a thick mist, a humidity of memory and presence. He experienced it as a kind of elation. Ruth was looking at him. He felt that he was in possession of something extremely valuable that she wanted. There were names written beside each of the buzzers. He stepped back and looked up at the building.

'It still looks like apartments.'

Ruth came over and stood beside him, looking at the buzzers. She was still silent, but then something occurred to her.

'You probably kissed her here for the first time.'

'No. That was in Central Park. By the reservoir.'

'You'd been in New York three years.' She was staring at him, making full eye contact, concentrating hard, putting together his story, possibly for the first time, as if it had only just now occurred to her that he was also somehow relevant to her.

'You were what? Twenty-six, twenty-seven? ... Mum was eighteen. You met her randomly on a train. You followed her.'

He hadn't seen his daughter like this in years, looking at him without hostility for a change but with curiosity, almost fascination. She was trying to make sense of the connotations, the random nature of things, how not just Miriam's life, the entire course of which was altered by randomly meeting him on the subway, but also her own existence depended on it. It was Miriam who was now looking at him, her mouth slightly open. Not her physical appearance, but everything about Ruth's body language, most of all her curiosity, a form of thirst. He stared, unable to speak, overcome by the presence of his wife, staring back at him through the eyes of his daughter.

'What did you say to her?' Ruth asked him. 'On the subway, I mean, when you met her? Tell me again.'

He smiled.

'I asked her what happened to her hands. Her left one had deep lines on it, grooves, from the cello, they looked painful. I asked her where she was studying, and she told me Juilliard, and she asked me what I was doing and I told her. There was no great mystery to it. I stayed on until 96th Street and got off with her. Talked to her all the way until we got...'

He looked around and said, There, pointing at a spot just outside the small knee-high fence that demarcated the outer border of the property.

'Right. There,' he said. 'Where we said goodbye.'

Ruth was silent and they both stared and at the same time moved towards the totally nondescript patch of sidewalk that he was pointing at, absorbed for a few moments by its imaginative stimulus and – for the pair of them if for nobody else on the planet – its historical resonance.

PART II

HE HADN'T BEEN back there in years. He had used the phone to keep in touch with her, though not exactly on a weekly basis. There was never any hint of how badly gone she was. He hadn't realized how easy it was for people to cover up that sort of thing. Confabulation is the technical term for it, an easily enough learned skill, where the individual can prattle away quite pleasantly and you have to be on the lookout to notice that they didn't answer your question with any degree of specificity, even if it was a factual one along the lines of where are you or who are you or who am I or what day or date is it today? His mother would get very irritated with anything that went along those lines and she would shake her head in frustration, and mutter to herself in German, which he of course didn't speak, a few strands of her long, now totally white hair hanging down over her face, surrounded by the full unglory of her filthy house.

That was the biggest shock, the state of the place, and the firmest endorsement of the diagnosis he and Miriam came to straight away upon seeing her for what was the first time since their wedding in Manhattan the previous summer. Now it seemed inconceivable that she had managed to make it there on her own. The flights, the check-in process, the luggage, the taxis to and from. In retrospect, there had been several points during that day when he had come across her sitting alone, appearing somewhat lost, but he had put it down to the overwhelming nature of the occasion, the fact that people were always coming up to her, introducing themselves, perfect strangers. He had to go looking for her, finding her near the stairwell in the place they'd rented, or on her own up on the small roof deck, the famous New Yorker sign visible some distance away behind her, brightly illuminated against what was a perfect summer's light blue. She had always been difficult, the old woman, proud, capable of acting spitefully. But here in front of them, the house was incontrovertible evidence. You couldn't move with the hoarded mess, the debris, the general filth of the place. He and Miriam stood in the front porch, overcome by the stench, stifling the nausea that stuck in their throats. His mother turned and walked away, leaving the front door wide open, no earthly clue who they were.

It was meant to be a quick visit. Two nights, then off to Vilnius in Lithuania, where Miriam's family had come from back in the day – or that part of the family which stimulated the historical imagination. The SS Einsatzgruppen and all that business. Operation Barbarossa. The Ostland. The Pripet Marshes. Yes, he'd been reading up on it in preparation, discovering within himself a modest scholarship that he hadn't known existed. Or perhaps he was trying to impress Miriam with how present he was all of a sudden with this newfound interest in her heritage. She had always spoken about going to that part of the world. Ever since she was a small child she'd been hearing about the place, to the extent that it had become almost mythical for her, so he surprised her with a trip. He also felt that he needed to make a gesture in her direction. His new career as an artist had taken off, and the last few months had been wild, hectic, glorious; they had hardly spent any time together, practically every night of the week there was something on, an opening, a party. He booked the trip using some of the new money he was making. Four days, returning by way of Warsaw. It would do them good to get away, a fresh start and all that. Miriam took the news with more reticence than he expected. The winter had been long, depressing, blocks of grey days with no sun visible, not even a shaft of morning light, nothing, just constant rain, God, London was bleak. Could they not go to Portugal?

They followed his mother into the kitchen, leaving their luggage on the front step. The state of the place was something to behold. Empty boxes and plastic bags and all manner of rubbish strewn across the floor, old cartons, long-rotted food that had hardened into indefinable objects, broken glass, a sour, sickening smell from somewhere, ammonia, waste, human, other. The old woman was already sitting in the armchair by the kitchen window, a path worn to it through the clutter, her eyes fixed outward on the garden, which was thickly overgrown. He and Miriam stood back from her like visiting dignitaries. Beneath her mound of clothes she was a skeleton. She wore a thick woollen jumper that looked familiar, threadbare in places, his long-dead father's. The kitchen around them had been ransacked, every drawer and cabinet emptied onto the floor, the countertops covered with trash, tinned food, some of the tins unopened. In the corner of the room the skirting board had rotted away and there was a large hole. The place was freezing. He reached for the light switch, but it didn't work. He mentioned London, the flight over. Mother, he said, but there was no reaction. Miriam went over to her and put her arms around her. The old woman didn't take her eyes off her garden. Miriam turned around and looked back at him; her eyes stayed on him until he looked away.

He suggested a hotel but Miriam responded with disbelief. He was always drawn to what was expedient, wasn't he? She walked away from him a few paces, then stood taking in the mess, blocking him out. She wanted to cry. Perhaps she was thinking about her father in New York, sitting in a similar room. Not ransacked in his case – on the contrary, it would be immaculate, his clothes pressed and laundered, the utilities working perfectly, of course. He'd be up at the crack of dawn, going hard at the world. He still ran his business. But the evenings would be quiet and the big house in Queens empty.

He went to the Spar to buy cleaning equipment. He didn't meet anyone on the way. The houses in the small cul-de-sac where his family home was had deteriorated, their façades blackened by neglect and by the damp fog that came off the Irish sea, their gardens not as unkempt as his mother's, but left mostly to nature all the same. Only a few cars were parked outside, and certainly no young people lived around here, that much was clear. Clontarf Road was a busy thoroughfare by comparison. The water a silver mirror, Bull Island barely visible through the thick mist. The shopkeeper was an Indian woman with a Dublin accent. She didn't recognize him, but one man coming into the shop did a double take then stood behind him in the queue, staring at the back of his neck. He'd become used to this type of attention recently. In London someone would come up to him on a daily basis, or just sit across from him on the Tube stealing glances at him, or baldly staring into his face, wondering why it was familiar. In the last few months he'd been appearing on television. An arts show that went out late on Friday nights on Channel 4. He'd met one of the producers at an opening and she had invited him to appear as a guest and now he was a regular. On the show they discussed art and politics and cultural issues. One of those red triangles was displayed at the start as a warning. They did shots and smoked on air. They were obnoxious and said the first things that came into their heads. He and the producer had a bit of a fling, nothing serious.

'You're Mrs Mateus's son.'

'Yes.'

The other man just stood there. Possibly this was the end of the conversation.

'You don't see her around the place any more. She used to be away off on her bicycle. Is she OK?'

'Fine. A bit under the weather. You know yourself how it is.'

The woman behind the counter was waiting for him. He could feel the man's eyes watching each item as he placed them on the counter. Bleach. Sponges. Various soaps and detergent. Two brushes. Rolls of kitchen paper. A mop and bucket. A bottle of wine. The whole lot came in at almost two hundred quid. They'd no big bags so he took it all in six or seven small ones.

Miriam wanted him to cancel the flights to Vilnius and get the money back from the airline. Instead he changed the dates, pushing everything back a week, which cost a hundred and fifty pounds. His argument was they had nothing to hurry back to London for. A month earlier he had finally had the courage to quit the advertising agency, so he could do pretty much what he wanted. For the first time in his life he was rolling in it, relatively speaking. And Miriam was only doing an Open University course. Sure you could do that from anywhere, just bring your books with you. Come on, it will do us good to get away.

Neither of them said anything for a while. Maybe she was thinking about it.

'Look,' he said, 'I'm sorry. I know the last few months have been a bit mad.'

She stared at him, then looked down at where he had placed his hand on her elbow. He took it away.

'Am I supposed to be impressed by that?' she said.

He cleared out the back bedroom first, his old childhood room, turning the mattress to find with relief that it was OK. They could sleep in here. The smell was only of damp. He opened the window. Miriam was downstairs on the phone to the electricity company, her voice coming up through the floorboards. He sat down on the mattress and looked around. Possibly he had been the last person to enter this room, ten or so years earlier, before heading to art school in Leeds. It was the only place that he could get into. He assumed they must not have even looked at the woeful portfolio he'd sent them.

There was a large dresser near the door. Strange that he had no memory of it, as if it had been parachuted in. He opened the top drawer, rummaged around. Junk. A box of cigars. Dry tissue paper. Matches. A stack of photographs, which were familiar to him now that he took them out and started to flick through them. Mostly black and white, his father's family, groups of smiling Germans, fair-haired children and adults, he could pick out his father in some of them.

The new money was art money. He'd got in with the Goldsmiths crowd who were beginning to make a big splash. He knew Carl Freedman vaguely through a college friend who had transferred there. Carl was a mate of Damien Hirst and was putting together a follow-up to the Freeze show which had been such a big hit for everyone. He'd run into him on the street one day and showed him his photos, a new technique he was using, something he'd learned at the agency. Carl thought they were cool and invited him to take part in the show. It was to be a group thing at Building One, the old biscuit factory in Bermondsey. Derek Landy was in it, Anya Gallaccio, and one or two of the others. Wolf knew Derek a little but that was it. He put in two of his 'geo' pieces, which he'd already moved on from. He had spent practically the whole time in New York working on them and hated them now. Digital reworkings of his photography, applying some of the new technology that was available. Everything sold. He got some of the press that went with it. There was another exhibition and then another one after that. For the past six months he had had a piece in the Whitechapel Gallery.

The hallway and kitchen areas were the worst. The stench was unbelievable, but it was hard to locate or specify. It was only partly human, an organic miasma which had embedded into the structure of the place, its feculent crust freshening when you scraped it. Astonishing how much junk she had gathered, as if she had taken whole deliveries of it. Sent away asking for it and waited for the trucks to arrive bearing it all. The old woman didn't resist in any way. She kept mostly to her spot by the kitchen window. Possibly she experienced the whole thing as a trauma, these strangers who had set about tearing up her home, banging on the walls, dividing everything into bin bags. What did they want with her? What violence did they intend to perpetrate?

Sometimes she spoke to them in German. This was something she had done even back in his childhood, seeming to forget that he didn't speak the mother tongue. The look of disappointment she'd give him then. His parents had always spoken English to each other, his father had insisted on it. We must speak English now, it's for the boy, Edith, we don't want him to have an accent! As a result he didn't speak a single word of German. They argued in that language though. For him, that's what German was for. A language that grown-ups fought in. It had the right tone for it.

Miriam worked a lot harder than he did. It wasn't even close. He just wanted to be done with the place and he couldn't understand the frenzy of her effort, its ferocity, where it was coming from. As far as he was concerned, it went way beyond the strict necessity of the situation. He stood over her as she kneeled on the floor, going at it with the head of a brush, the long handle removed, pressing down straight-armed on the brushhead, jerking it forward and back, forward and back. She was in a sleeveless top, the muscles of her shoulders contracting, her hair wet. He wanted her to slow down, to take it easy.

'You do know we're only going to be selling it.'

She paused to recognize his voice, that seemed to come

from outside whatever trance she was in, but then kept going.

'I mean, it's not as if we can leave her here on her own anyway, right? And we're going to need the money for wherever we put her into.'

But still she continued. He stood looking down on her. On and on she went, sometimes emitting little grunting noises as she pressed down into the ground, literally scrubbing the floors, then pouring boiling water on them, bleach, taking another crack at them, scalding every inch, every kitchen tile, every piece of crockery. Between times she sat exhausted on the back step staring at the overgrown garden. The joints of her hands ached, her hips, her knees, her back. He watched her from a safe distance. It was never the right time to talk to her. There was a home in Clontarf, not far. Or at least there had been when he was growing up. It may have been privatized by now, or turned into apartments, he could check. It used to be run by the nuns, a frightening grey building on a slight incline which looked out at the rough water. He had to walk past it every day on his way to school. But it was as if Miriam didn't hear him. When he had finished talking she didn't say anything, continuing to stare out at the garden. This distance between them worried him. He'd overdone it the past few months. He'd been using too much cocaine, even to the point of developing a slight reliance on it. Anything that was going on he was up for. He didn't want to turn down any possibility. This was his chance, his big break. Miriam didn't know about the producer. But that was no big deal anyway, it didn't mean anything, just another part of this new life he was trying out. It was for both their sakes really, he'd never get it out of his system otherwise. He'd already made up his mind to end it as soon as he got back to London. The producer herself was under no illusions. Her father was in the House of Lords and she seemed to know everyone. Anyway, he was thinking he'd go and check out the home. See what the situation was. She could stay here. At first Miriam didn't say anything. What a relief then when she asked him to bring her back a coffee.

When he was gone she walked around the house, a little freer. It was hard to pinpoint exactly why she found it difficult to be in his presence right now, why he irritated her so much. Up and down the hallway she walked, as if she owned the place, which in a way she did now, into the living room at the front, all of which she had cleared more or less by herself. Physical work was not his strong point. She remembered when this was a source of amusement for her. She stood in the hallway listening to the silence. A small snoring from her mother-in-law, fast asleep in her chair in the kitchen. Or was it the breeze coming through the broken window? It was amazing how the old woman had blended into her neglected surroundings. Miriam envied her that. Sometimes you forgot completely that she was there.

It was still a nursing home, although the nuns weren't to be seen anywhere. The inside of it, the hallway anyhow, was a pleasant surprise, bright and clean, the walls a calm yellow. A piano was being played somewhere. A woman asked him if he was OK and told him to take a seat, indicating the chairs arranged against the wall. He looked at the paintings, of choppy water and clouds, Howth in the background. It took a while for the woman to return. She gave him a brochure, although the glossy photographs in it seemed to be of some other place. We have different packages, she said. Here, I have the more up-to-date info on a separate printout. She went to her computer. Again it took her ages to return.

The house had no memory either. That was it. She hadn't been able to put her finger on it before. But it was as if no family had ever lived here. There were no photographs. No framed images of Wolf's father, or of anyone else for that matter. No keepsakes, mementoes, not even the smallest trinket. Nothing whose continued presence could be put down to sentiment. There were no old toys that Wolf would have played with, his – I don't know – wooden cars or figurines. Whatever it was that little boys played with then. No schoolbooks or colouring jotters. It was possible they were all boxed away in the attic, but that seemed doubtful. Anyway, it was good that they didn't have to make any decisions. It was all recent junk, with nothing that could be described as having sentimental value. It could all be thrown out.

Whereas in her father's house there was no getting away from the past. It was all over the place, staring down from the walls at them through the eyes of the long-dead, still in their clothes from the shtetl, some of which appeared almost ornamental, doll-like, especially those of the young. They wouldn't have had a word of English between them, whoever these people were, wherever they were from. Kiev. Belarus. Vilnius. The far kitchen wall was her wall. (The other one belonged to her brother Isaac, it was smaller and the AC vent came in there, making it smaller still. It was always a bone of contention, yet another thing for Isaac to whine about.) Marks drawn in pencil, dates beside them, told what height she had been exactly when. Her father had left space to the side for more lines. This would be for the grandchildren. He had left a ridiculously big space, for an entire wall of grand-children – how many did he think she'd have? And it seemed that every scribble she ever did was cut out and taped there, several of them even framed, every Polaroid that had ever been taken of her and her little friends at some party. The sun a constant fixture, unlike now. In the corner a small cab-inet containing the ceremonial plates from her bat mitzvah, the candlesticks she had received as a gift and the hand-dyed tallis an older cousin, Linda, the feminist in the family, had given her. The top shelf containing the Elijah's cup they used at Passover, she painted it blue and white, the colours of Israel. All these things would be re-used for the grand-children. Yes yes the grandchildren. There he goes again. The noise there will be with all of them, especially on Shabbat, which of course they would have in her father's house every

Friday night, the walls would be coming down with all the singing, and it would be the same for all of the holidays – Pesach, Rosh Hashanah, Sukkot, and Hanukkah of course.

Yes, a trial run, say a weekend, would be a possibility. Although, to be honest, it can be disruptive for the individual, to come and go like that, depending on their, eh, status. We would need to get an assessment done. Has she been in hospital recently? Will you put down the details of her GP in this section, please? Does she take any medication? What about a medical card? Does she have VHI coverage? Some plans provide for care, you see. It's OK for now, but we would need all this information. You're better off taking the form away with you and filling it out properly. One thing you could do is call the local surgery and ask them if your mother is a patient of theirs. Explain the situation – they're usually very good about it. This coming weekend might be pushing it. We would have to check. It may work. It depends on whether we could get the medical assessment done. By the way, if you're looking to sell the property my advice to you would be to get started on that as soon as possible, especially if you're, eh, depending on it. Things move very slowly around here. We can recommend some local auctioneers.

That part of the Passover story where Moses goes to plead his case to Pharaoh and Pharaoh thinks that actually Moses has a fair point. As far back as she can remember she was confused by this passage when they read it aloud from the Haggadah every year during the Seder. She has always suspected that it represented the first moment of doubt for her. In this passage Pharaoh seems fairly benevolent actually, as he listens to what Moses is saying to him. Quite the wise king, he mulls it over with his advisers. The Hebrews have done really well for him, they've never given him any trouble, and he appears to be really thinking about Moses's proposal, giving the request some serious consideration. But just when it looks like he's headed in that direction, and a peaceful solution might be found, God intervenes to, quote unquote, *harden Pharaoh's heart*. The atmosphere in the room changes quite suddenly. Pharaoh is now angry, he denounces these ungrateful Hebrews. Moses must have been lucky to escape with his life, probably he had to run out of the great hall, past the guards, Pharaoh's furious voice shouting after them to stop him, find him, bring him back at once. It is billed as an inevitability then that over the next few weeks the plagues will start to arrive – the plague of water turned to blood, of frogs, to be followed by that of lice or gnats, then the plague of flies, the plague of livestock, of boils, of hail, of locusts, the plague of darkness, before the most famous and hideous one of them all – it was so strange, she always thought, that we celebrate it, that we name our most important holiday after it, after such unbelievable cruelty that was the murder of the firstborns, with a knife or however it was done, whatever creatures were sent to do it, she pictured hideous little things, psychotic angels, winged demons with machetes, who were given specific instructions of course to 'pass over' certain houses, those whose occupants were tipped off in advance to smear across their front door the blood of a lamb, and from whom all Jews were now descended. Was it really so glorious? Or so justified? Surely if God had intervened to, quote unquote, *harden Pharaoh's heart*, then clearly Pharaoh had lost agency in the decision? What responsibility did he bear? Why did nobody else appreciate this point which was so obvious to her? She must have been ten or eleven when this thought began to gnaw at her. She brought it up at many Passovers but never once got a good answer to her question. How precocious, they said. And her so cute and wearing such cute things! Such a child, a girl too! Oy vey! Questioning the grown-ups, even Uncle Lenny, who was a bit of a scholar on these matters and tended to have the final word with his spectacles and his wisdom as he folded and unfolded his handkerchief. And still they never answered her. Sometimes she thought that everything started there, that small thought which became a far bigger thought, and before you knew it she was living in London, more or less in exile, married to a gentile whom she doesn't see from one end of the day to the other. And her father. Her brother. How *angry* they are at her. They barely speak to her. She had put it down at least partially to the male pride. But more and more in recent months the question seems to have arisen, very quietly and very insistently, just like the Pharaoh thing. The only difference being that she has been even less clear about the answer, the question of exactly whose heart had been, quote unquote, *hardened*. Up until recently she had always assumed that it was theirs.

It was surprising how much the old woman complied with being bathed. There was no shower, so they left her to sit in the water which he made luxurious with balm and oil and baby's bubble bath. He felt less strangeness than he would have imagined confronted by his mother's body. Her underclothes were thickly soiled, to the point of not really smelling all that badly. They binned everything she wore. He took a taxi to the Dunnes in Raheny to buy her robes, jumpers and a thick, comfortable tracksuit. Miriam sponged her while he stood back, his wife's hands clenching the water out, the musculature on her upper arms mesmerizing him in the dim candlelight, a pietà of daughterly duty. He couldn't help but be impressed by it, as she took her time and set the clenched sponge to the thin skin of the old woman's skeleton. They took her out, dried her and sat her by the fire. It hadn't been lit in years. The draught in the chimney was the spirits being shooed out. Miriam stared into the flames. He couldn't fathom the rage of her sadness, that right now she regretted absolutely everything. The old woman was just as mesmerized. Sometimes it seemed that she understood perfectly what was going on. He said he'd go out and pick up a Chinese. Miriam barely responded. When he returned with the food he was the only one who ate any of it.

He had drunk most of the wine. When he woke the next morning, she was already at it. She was sitting on a chair she'd taken out to the back of the house, the garden gnarled and almost up to the level of the fence. A smell of fresh coffee. A plastic bag on the counter. She had already been to the shop. He poured himself a glass of water from the tap then joined his wife outside. Despite his hangover he wanted to give the impression that he was all business. The GP was coming today. He had the forms ready. There was a list of auctioneers to contact. But Miriam cut him off. We'll go on this little trip of yours, she said. I've been thinking about it. I want to go to Vilnius.

On the Friday morning they booked a taxi. It was a wheel-chair taxi, even though they didn't have a wheelchair and his mother was able to walk to it and get in and out with minimal assistance. He filled a suitcase with the new things he'd bought for her, the robe, the tracksuit, the loose warm clothes and thick socks and men's underwear, big cotton jocks that would go halfway down the old woman's legs, a tartan-coloured toilet bag, the essential toiletries. The taxi waited while they guided her up the ramp of the old grey building in Clontarf. The sun was out and shining very brightly. It was cold and the clouds moved with extraordi-nary speed across the sky. The water that he turned and looked out on from the elevated hill of the nursing home was choppy and the whole world was silent except for the legion of extremely loud gulls a fair distance away. He couldn't imagine it being any other way. The people at the home moved quickly, radiating competence. They clearly wanted rid of them, so that they could get her into a routine. His mother didn't seem to notice anything amiss. That was how it was going to be now and he didn't feel bad about it. Mainly because he knew that she herself would have understood. It was the logical thing to do and she was always a very logical, pragmatic person.

The same taxi took them to the airport. They made the departure gate just in time. On the plane Miriam stared out the window while he read the Lonely Planet guide to Lithuania. She didn't turn around once the entire way to Stansted, where they had to lay over for four hours. He'd brought some of his other books too, about the Holocaust obviously, the war period. Nothing else about that region's past was remotely of interest to him, it didn't even occur to him that it could be. He wanted to show Miriam that he was engaged, so it was a little irritating that she didn't seem to notice. If he didn't know better he would have thought she had no interest in this trip of theirs. He'd assumed she'd be impressed by his new knowledge. After a while he stopped glancing at her. He only flicked through the books then. Christ, the 1930s and '40s were a bleak time to be alive. He could practically hear the rain on the pages, the misery that was everywhere. In Stansted they ate at one of the featureless restaurants, there was nothing else to do. A young woman, a girl really, sat beside them and he noticed her straight away, the atmosphere changed by the fact that he couldn't stop looking at her. She wasn't travelling anywhere, it looked like she was on her lunch break. He wondered where she worked. Miriam picked up the Lonely Planet and turned to the pages with the maps.

'You know,' she said, 'I have no clue where Lithuania even is. It's just an idea that's been in my head all these years.'

After a few minutes the girl's lunch break was over and he watched her as she walked down the corridor, no doubt relieved to be away from his gawking.

Miriam was looking at him.

'What is it that you expect to see differently each time?' she asked.

He pretended to not know what she was talking about.

'No, I'm serious. What do you look at first?'

She sat back and folded her arms. There was a man standing not far from them, a mobile phone to his ear. Miriam made a point of looking at him.

'For me it's the shoulders,' she said. 'Especially if he's tall.'

They got into Vilnius around two in the afternoon. An old Mercedes taxi brought them to their hotel, a family-run one near the centre. It was in the Lonely Planet, the mid-range section. Checking in, the man was friendly but Miriam was uninterested, frankly a little rude. She used her married name, which otherwise she used only erratically. No, she said, they didn't need help with their bags. Where was a good place to get a meal? No, no, a meal. A meal. Food! Dinner! She had no patience with this man and walked off, irritated. After a minute Wolf joined her. He didn't ask her if she was all right. Next door was the recommended option. No doubt it was all under the same ownership, I'm sure they try to get everyone to go there. Once they dropped their bags up in the room they went out and stood in front of the hotel, situated on a semi-busy street. God, Vilnius was a grim place. The airport, the taxi in, right now as they stood in a light drizzle, old-style Eastern European cars going by. It felt like they were the only visitors, the only outsiders. The sky was low and heavy and this seemed permanent, somehow structural, even though the man at reception had told them they'd recently had weeks of 'almost summer'.

They took it easy the first night, a few drinks in the dive bar on the other side of the restaurant which they didn't bother with after all. Miriam drank almost as much as he did, gin, neither of them were hungry, then back to the hotel. There'd been a mistake and they'd been given a double and a single bed. When he came out of the bathroom Miriam was already sleeping on the single, leaving him the double. In the morning she was already up and gone. She must have gone out somewhere to get some breakfast.

They walked around the centre of Vilnius aimlessly, mostly in silence. They had a few quasi-landmarks to follow up on which Miriam had been hearing about since she was a small child from her father. Avram had never been to Vilnius, so the descriptions were non-specific and generic, handed down through the family in the context of legend or myth: a large red-bricked building near the main square, 'as big as factory', and which could have been any one of several places they stood in front of on that first day, trying to imagine it as it once had been, a prosperous bakery feeding half the town, and belonging to Avram's grandfather, and in the family for generations before that. One day Avram's father, nineteen years old, just married, got caught up in one of the mini-pogroms which seemed to be erupting more frequently. He escaped with his life and decided to leave – he and his wife didn't have any children yet. He tried to convince the rest of the family, his father especially, but also his stepmother and her five children from her previous marriage, who were all younger than him, and – according to another component of the family myth – much favoured by the stepmother. Whatever he had witnessed applied only to thugs and degenerates, his stepmother said. That's who the dead must have been. We are a prosperous old family. Your father is on the town council. Everybody is our customer, friend even. Judge, officer, policeman, Christian priest even. We have too much here. Where would we go besides? To the desert to just die?

It would have been great to locate the bakery. Wolf and Miriam stood in front of one of the most likely buildings for a long time, searching it for any markers which hinted at a previous identity, an engraving on the front glass, letters carved into the wall on the bottom bricks, but finding only a word they couldn't make out and the year 1921, the iron railings' forge mark. There was no family name or anything specific. It was now some sort of office building, with what looked like shabby apartments on the top floors. They checked several similar buildings. He photographed them all.

They continued walking around with no particular sense of direction or orientation, starting mostly at the centre of the city, but then extending out in more or less random directions. He kept pausing to photograph some fixture or fitting in the railings or cement or any building which had the impression of age and time about it, which amounted to a large number of structures. He had the guidebook opened at the section of city maps of different magnifications and was constantly calling out bits and pieces of information, but Miriam responded blankly or only in a minimal fashion.

She was like that all evening. They had an early dinner back in the place next to the hotel. The waitress was beautiful and he knew that Miriam saw him looking at her but also that she couldn't care less. The waitress had jet black hair and looked at him with a hint of a smile. Miriam asked her a question about the specials and the waitress was terse. No. We cannot do. The menu is the menu. A gold crucifix dangled from her neck. The top two buttons of her white shirt were open and Wolf glimpsed what she was wearing underneath. She walked away from their table, Wolf watching her as she went across the room. At first Miriam didn't say anything.

'What?'

Still she didn't say anything, that strange look on her face.

'What?' he repeated. She made him nervous when she was like this.

'I really went all in with you, didn't I?'

'We both did.'

'No,' she said, taking up her gin. He'd never seen her drink like this. 'No we didn't.'

After a few minutes the waitress returned with some bread and a jug of water. As she leaned over the large crucifix hung down again, catching the light of the small candle. For a second it was ablaze. He asked her to bring them another round of drinks. Miriam didn't protest.

'I hate this place,' she said when the waitress was out of range.

'You're imagining it.'

A burst of light suddenly appeared in the window out of nowhere. It took him a second or two to realize it was artificial, from a truck which had pulled in to park in the alleyway beside the hotel. A loud beeping noise sounded and the light turned abruptly off.

He told the proprietor of the hotel that they were going to the old town, was it far?

'Old town? Nice,' he said. 'Art museum, fancy restaurant, many shops for woman to keep her happy. Ha ha ha!'

'We're looking for the ghetto,' Miriam said. 'The Jewish ghetto.'

'Ghetto?' the man said. 'I don't know "ghetto". Shops and restaurant, yes, but ghetto, no. But you want, I get you taxi. Very good price.'

Miriam walked off and the man looked at Wolf and gave a little shrug. Wolf thanked him and went after her.

The taxi brought them to Niemiecka Street, a large tree-lined boulevard with cafés and restaurants. It was overcast but not raining and people were sitting out at tables drinking espressos, having business lunches. It was more cosmopolitan than the area they'd been tramping around all morning. They walked up and down the street for a while, although it was more like an avenue than a mere street. He kept the guide-book open, orientating the maps in relation to the old ghetto areas which he had outlined in pen on one of them. He was able to explain some of the history to Miriam, but she barely listened to him as he rabbited on, listing off the cross streets, telling her that this was it, this had been the centre of it all, right here, this exact place where they were walking right now. There would have been a wooden fence here, delineating the perimeter. He had seen pictures, old photographs, in one of his other books – there was one point of entry to each ghetto, and a separate point of exit at the other end. Miriam was barely listening to him, lagging behind him, so every now and again he had to pause and wait for her to catch up. At one corner she stopped.

'Let's go up here,' she said.

'Zydu Street,' he said, looking at the sign and down at his map. 'This was part of Ghetto 2.' But Miriam was already walking up the street. He followed after her and they went along it until they got to Stikliu Street, where Miriam stopped outside a shop. She was staring at the ground, her face given a golden tinge by the storefront behind her. The shop window was full of Baltic amber, Lithuania's most famous product. He knew all about that too – the books frequently referenced it and there were shops selling it all over the place. Apparently the most valuable pieces contained some organic matter, a trapped fly preserved down the millennia, a transparent tomb that you could wear around your neck. The area was quiet and the cobbled streets very narrow. Miriam was looking at him and her expression was strange and hard to read, a little antagonistic. She took a deep breath and looked around her and then smiled at him. Let's go back to the hotel, she said. It looks like it might rain.

The next day they got a taxi out to the Hertz office at the airport and hired a car. They followed the main Warsaw road until they found the signs for Paneriai. The weather had worsened overnight and it rained constantly. The sky was low and heavy, with barely any light getting through. The forest was perpetually in the middle distance, dark and dense and endless, a sleeve of nondescript lowlands separating it from the narrow country roads threading many thin small towns together, heralded well in advance by cheap hoardings in Cyrillic, advertising things that didn't exist any more. There were no signs for the memorial and it took a while for them to find it, off a side road which led further into the forest. Eventually they came to a small empty car park. A large sign in black stone lying on the grass verge said 'Paneriu memorialas'. They got out of the car and looked over at it. There was evidence of vandalism on the sign, graffiti in bright orange, some writing in what he guessed to be Polish and a large swastika, spray-painted. The loose gravel of the car park crunched as they walked on it, through some gates to a small museum building which was closed. The sign said that it was a subsidiary of the Vilna Gaon Jewish State Museum. They peered through the window and read the laminated information sheet on the glass-fronted noticeboard. They had come during 'off-peak' and the opening hours were sparse. He looked around to see Miriam standing back a few paces. She was staring at the ground, her face empty, grief-stricken.

'What's wrong?'

'It's also Shabbos,' she said.

Her tone was shocked. How could she not have thought of this? Here of all places to forget it. She stared at him, completely stunned. He put his hand on her shoulder. It's easy to get disorientated when you're away, he said. She turned and looked bitterly at him, with some anger, but then her expression changed and he saw the sadness in her eyes and he put his arms around her and she did not resist.

They walked through the car park and along a tarmac path which led further into the forest for a few hundred yards until they came across a clearing just beyond the first boundary of dark trees. It was nondescript and unheralded and at first he thought that the area they were looking for must be further on. Miriam, walking just behind him, came to a standstill. Ahead were two large indentations in the ground. He moved towards them and Miriam slowly followed. The indentations were grass covered and neatly kept, benign. If you didn't know better they could be mistaken for the well-tended hollows of a golf course. He went to the edge. Wooden steps led down into the hollows but neither he nor Miriam descended them. They stood for a while, Miriam fixed to the ground where she was standing a bit further back. He wandered around the circumference of one of the pits, every now and again looking back at the dense forest that surrounded them, silent and watching. They could make out the other two pits in another clearing a little way off which was connected by the path. Miriam came forward and stared down into the pit. According to what they had just read on the information sheet in its glass case, the pits were shallower now than they would have been at the time, the level having risen afterwards from the ash and earth put back on top to partially fill them in. Originally the pits had been dug by the Russians, who intended to use this place as a fuel depot, presumably because it was near the railway line. Large tanks or containers of different sizes could be lowered into the ground and filled with the fuel. But they never got that far, and by the time the Germans arrived they found the empty pits, unused. The pits simply lay there, open, as if waiting to be put to some purpose.

'I can't decide if it's easy to imagine it or impossible,' Wolf said, standing on the edge of the grass pit.

'It's easy,' Miriam said.

The rain strengthened and made the day darker. They stood for a further short while and then wandered around with no great intent, keeping to the clear areas where the sky was at least visible. At one point he left Miriam and walked over to face the forest which seemed to extend forever into its own silence. He had never seen anything as impenetrable as this frightening mesh of trees. The same trees since the age of Christ, they contained the memory of the Dark Ages, had witnessed everything, all time's hordes passing through in their animal furs. Europe's soul was in there, her pure black blood seeping into the roots from the soil. After a while they moved in silence back in the direction of the car park and then to Vilnius. The next day brought torrential, unrelenting rain. They didn't leave the hotel at all. At lunch Miriam continued the pattern of drinking a lot, at least by her standards. She must have had four or even five Kir royales. They were in bed by 7 p.m. The next day they flew back to Dublin.

PART III

I

HE FOUND HIMSELF seated at the middle of a long table, his back to the wall, no way out without everyone having to get up. The room was familiar but he couldn't think from where exactly. The walls were covered with framed pictures, some colour, some black and white, children's drawings, many of them were just scribbles, some of them had even been framed. An elderly couple arrived late. They seemed to know everyone and took up the two seats directly across from him. The man nodded at him but the woman didn't acknowledge Wolf, which he thought was rude. The lady at the head of the table got up to speak. Judy was her name. She wanted to welcome everyone, she said, to what was, technically anyway, the second night of Rosh Hashanah, which they had had to put off for a couple of nights for the sake of Isaac and Max. She had just received a text that their plane had landed, so why didn't they just go ahead and get started? I don't have the Hebrew chops that Avram has, she said, so let's just say that I'm happy we are all here together, and I really hope this coming year is better than the last one, that's for sure. There was a rather sudden and surprisingly deep silence as she leaned on her outstretched arm, her head bowed, momentarily emotional. The man beside her held her wrist, probably it was her husband. She turned and dabbed at her eyes and said, God, I still can't believe she's gone, and that was followed by more silence. It took a while for the conversation level to rise and Wolf listened to various strands of it on either side of him without quite catching any of it. Dishes full of food were sent down the table. The meal proceeded quickly, with bread and various symbolic food items – apple and honey, star fruit, pomegranate – being passed around. He noticed his daughter Ruth was seated down to his left, on the other side of the table, surrounded by young people. Wolf was surprised to see her there. He gave her a wave but she only gave him a funny look back. She was dressed in the same manner as her mother, a long dress down to her feet, her full, thick hair unfurled, rich like a mane. He couldn't take his eyes off her, she looked so grown up. Avram was down that end also. He looked tired and kept dropping off to sleep, much to the amusement of the five or six young people who surrounded him. Wolf couldn't have put a name to any of them and he was happy to retreat back into himself and be ignored. It didn't take long for the meal to move on to the main course. It came as a surprise when the man opposite leaned forward to speak to him.

'When do you head back to London?'

Wolf mumbled something and went straight back to eating. But then he wondered if he'd been rude.

'Have you ever been?' he said to the man, but it was just out of politeness. What did he care if the man had or hadn't?

Now it was the man's turn to be confused. He just stared back at Wolf.

'Yes, I think I mentioned to you the other night that we lived there at one time. For my residency. At King's.'

'Residency,' Wolf said, and for some reason he laughed. 'That sounds nice.'

The man was looking at him.

'It was a good time for us.'

'What do you do for a living?' Wolf asked him. Again he was just being polite.

The man looked at him like he was taken aback. Wolf could feel himself getting irritated.

'I'm a physician,' the man said. 'A cardiologist.'

The woman beside him was also looking at Wolf. She seemed interested in him now. Wolf noted the blue and white skullcap she was wearing. He didn't think he'd ever seen a woman wear one before. He was going to ask her about it, but the moment passed and in any case he didn't like the vibe he was getting from this couple. They looked at each other, before the man was spoken to by Allen.

'So, Mort, I hear you were asked to do the drash last week.'

'Oh, is that so?' the woman at the head of the table said. 'What was the Torah portion?'

'It was from Numbers, right, Morty? I want to say Numbers,' the woman in the blue and white skullcap said.

Wolf was aware that he was retreating back into himself. He barely said anything else for the rest of the meal, just drank his water and the spare bit of wine that came his way. What sort of a dinner party was this anyway? Friends of Miriam. Clearly from the Jewish community. These occasions could be hit-and-miss, sometimes OK and sometimes excruciating. Even she didn't seem to be enjoying herself all that much. She was seated down to his left, on the other side of the table, surrounded by a bunch of giddy teenagers who, by the looks of things, were irritating her no end. It wasn't like Miriam, who generally had infinite patience, even where he was concerned. He had zero connection to these people and it was a struggle to remind himself who any of them were, but he allowed himself to give up that struggle and simply go with the feeling, to feel no sense of panic, just a sort of buoyancy. He could have been any age in his life, at any point in it. The absurdity of the whole thing made him laugh. Miriam was looking at him now. He laughed again and sensed people looking at each other, at him, but when he looked up nobody in fact was paying him any attention. They were talking over him and around him and he had no idea what they were talking about.

2

THEY WERE NEARLY finished with dinner when the front door of the house opened and a shout came from the hallway: 'I hope you all have saved some chicken soup for me, you greedy slobs!'

There was no mistaking that voice, and Wolf recognized it immediately. It had the effect of a slap, causing him to sit up in his chair. He could hear suitcases being wheeled along the wooden floors, and a second or two later his brother-in-law Isaac appeared in front of them at the head of the table, behind where Allen was sitting, followed by his partner Max.

'Greetings, mi familia!' Isaac shouted, half singing it. Judy got up and went over and hugged her cousin.

'It feels like we left Barcelona a week ago!' Isaac said, 'and oh my God are we so totally amped for some good kosher wine and gefilte fish or what?'

Isaac stood with his arm around Judy's waist, looking out over the entire table.

'Shana Tova, you crowd of ruffians,' he said. 'Hey, you actually all look not so unpresentable.'

'Isaac,' Avram said from the opposite end of the table, 'come and say hello properly.'

'Yes, mein Vater,' Isaac said, and he began working his

way along the side of the table opposite Wolf, greeting every-one individually. His partner Max stayed where he was, Judy beside him.

The teenagers in particular were excited to see Isaac. Even Ruth was looking at him, smiling. It wasn't just his person-ality, there was the fact that Isaac was vaguely associated with the world of celebrity, at least in their eyes, given his profes-sion as an opera singer, and that he was always on the verge of 'making it'. On top of that, one of his college friends was the pop star Sophie Appleton, who even Wolf had heard of. They did seem genuinely close. Isaac often accompanied her on the red carpet, and even appeared in one of her music videos, as a love interest who jilts her and then comes running back. Isaac had spent most of the past twenty years in Europe, Italy mainly, but recently Spain. He was 'on the circuit', whatever that meant, getting occasional employment as an understudy in various productions, although as far as Wolf could tell he had mostly worked as a waiter in a restaurant in Barcelona entirely staffed by fully trained singers. Apparently they broke into song as they served your food. For years Wolf had been hearing that Isaac needed to get older so that his voice would mature, but surely he must have reached that point by now. He was in his mid-forties and, looking at him as he made his way along the table, he had a bit of a middle-age paunch. It sure seemed to Wolf that his days of promise were behind him, at least on first glance, which most of the time is all you need, especially if you knew like he did what to look for.

Isaac moved along the line, finally getting to Ruth. As Ruth was embraced by her uncle there was a change in the atmosphere. They remained like that for a long time without saying anything.

Isaac was the one member of his wife's family whom Wolf had seen in recent times. Isaac had stayed with them the previous March, spending time with Miriam and also Ruth, taking her on trips into the city. He had even accompanied Miriam on one or two of her treatment visits into King's. Wolf had kept in the background on those occasions. He knew his brother-in-law's opinion of him. There was in the younger man a streak that you could almost call moralistic, even if it took you a while to spot. That excessive extroversion, the ostensible glamour of his profession, the international way of life, et cetera, could make you easily miss what was in reality an old-fashioned conscientiousness, a high degree of discipline and an appetite for work, and a quite conservative home life. He and Max had been together for fifteen, sixteen years and both of them wore identical rings on the ring fingers of their right hands. Isaac had studied at Juilliard, just as Miriam had once – both on scholarships, Isaac's a full one – but, in contrast to Miriam, he had stuck at it. He won the Leonard Bernstein Prize in his sophomore year and was written about in the *New York Times* as one to watch. The three of them hung out quite a bit when Miriam and Wolf had first got together. Isaac was also living on the Upper West Side, although he spent a fair bit of time in the family home in Queens, more time than Wolf would have expected, given that only Avram was there, and also because Isaac knew a lot of people and gave the impression of being very sociable and always having a ton of things going on. It was easy to assume that that's who he was, the person at the centre of things, the extrovert with a thousand friends, but in reality Isaac was a bit of a loner and totally dependent on Miriam, who felt all the time that she had to mind him and not just watch out for him but also watch what she said around him, so as not to offend him, which was easily done. Initially Wolf had assumed that there would be some sort of outsider kinship between them, the gay and the gentile. It took him a while to realize that if anything Isaac was more of a traditionalist than Miriam, and more religious. When they went out for meals he insisted on eating only in places that were strictly kosher. On several occasions he had also heard Isaac express views that were stridently pro-Israel and intolerant.

'I miss her so much,' he was saying to Ruth after he finally pulled himself away. Ruth was staring at the floor. Wolf knew that his daughter was mortified by this public display, whereas with Isaac he would have expected no less. He used his forearm to wipe away his tears. The grief was no doubt genuine, but with him there was always a performance aspect, the pro's knowledge of where the audience was and which of his profiles they were getting. Wolf looked around the table. Judy had reached out and was holding Allen's hand, their eyes gleaming.

Isaac was also the only one of Miriam's family who had made it over to London for the cremation ceremony. No doubt if there had been a burial service they would all have travelled.

It had been made plain to Wolf in the hours after her death that Miriam should be buried whole, according to the Jewish tradition, so that her body could remain intact for the afterlife. Judy had called him about it the night Miriam had died. He had already spoken to her earlier that day, and on several occasions from the hospital, telling her about Miriam and what was happening, giving her updates so that she could keep the rest of the family informed, explaining it all urgently, barely taking a breath. Now – after the raw and numbing finality of things – she was calling him back not on her own behalf but on Avram's.

'Listen, Wolf,' Judy said, 'I know you have to do what you feel is right. Personally, my own feeling is we've lost her and—'

She was crying now and had to pause for a moment before continuing.

'It's just that her father is old school. To that generation . . .'

Wolf could hear Avram in the background. He sounded distraught and was shouting. It sounded like they were holding him back from the phone.

'My daughter must have a Jewish burial!' he shouted. 'Tell him, tell him, Judy!'

Wolf didn't have strong feelings about the burial. What they wanted would have been fine by him. He could not see himself visiting a physical grave, could not imagine such a thing giving him solace, quite the opposite actually. In any case, he knew by then that he wouldn't be around long enough for those visits. There was even in him the small sentimentality of wanting to be buried with Miriam, but these were not strong thoughts or ones that he dwelt on with any great seriousness. The point was that Miriam herself hadn't wavered an ounce in her certainty. Nor could she have been more specific.

'Bring me back to New York,' she had told him. 'In the event of things. I want to be cremated. Spread my ashes on the Hudson. The Upper West Side on a sunny day. My birthday perhaps, I quite like the symmetry of that.'

She'd laughed when she said it, as if the thought calmed her. This was four months before she died, around the time the doctors decided to change her chemotherapy regimen. The three of them were sitting in their back garden looking up at the sun. Ruth started crying. It was early summer. All around them in the back gardens of their neighbours' houses, separated by wooden fences over head height, were the voices of children excited about the prospect of summer. The air was thick and warm and full. They were playing some game with water.

'Judy,' he said with firmness over the phone, 'Miriam was clear about what she wanted. She doesn't want to be buried in the ground. She asked me to promise her. I want to do as she wished. I want to do this for her. As her husband.'

'I understand,' Judy said.

He could imagine Avram's retort once the phone was hung up: 'Now he wants to be a good husband?! Now?!'

The other reason nobody had travelled to London was the suddenness of things. She was here and then she was gone. In the morning she had developed a new symptom – breathlessness, even when she sat straight up in bed and didn't move or exert herself. She woke him up to tell him about it, she was almost amused at first, as if she had made a small worthwhile discovery. But as the day progressed so did the symptom, until her panic became pronounced. The doctors in casualty told him there was no fluid to drain. Initially he thought this must be a good thing, but their manner suggested otherwise.

'There's nothing reversible,' the registrar replied, not looking at him directly.

They admitted her, and as evening replaced afternoon the amount of oxygen she required increased. Then night followed as quickly. They had no time to talk and Miriam was panicked. He wanted everything to stop for an hour so that they could gather themselves and think things through – to call a timeout, just as they do in sports, where you can raise your hand to the sideline or make some signal to the referee to say that you need a break. But there was none of that. There was no stopping and there was no stepping back.

By the time Isaac arrived in London from Barcelona and made it to the hospital Miriam was already in the morgue. Wolf met him at the front of the hospital.

'Where is she?' was the first thing Isaac said, getting out of the taxi.

Wolf brought his brother-in-law down in the freight lift, the most direct way. Isaac was hysterical. His face was red and his body was trembling as if he was in withdrawal. Miriam was on a trolley, a sheet laid over her. Wolf didn't want to see her again and stood by the door. He was afraid of what his memory would cling to. More and more it seemed to have a mind of its own, indiscriminate, with no sense or logic to it. Isaac's head and shoulders went under the sheet as he held on to her. The sheet rustled and a sobbing emanated from it. The undertaker appeared at the door and Wolf stood back and then went outside. It was only afterwards, after the undertakers had prepared Miriam's body to be taken away, that Isaac came outside and spoke to him.

'Why didn't you fucking call me sooner?'

Wolf looked back at him as if across a large distance. He was still shocked by the pace of things, and Isaac's question seemed valid but unanswerable.

'You,' Isaac continued. 'You . . .' He stopped at that and just shook his head. He stopped himself from crying before turning once more towards Wolf.

'SHE WAS MY SISTER!' he screamed, as loud as he could into Wolf's face. Wolf just looked back at him, saying nothing.

Now when Isaac came out of his long embrace with Ruth he reached over and extended his hand towards Wolf and glanced at him briefly. Wolf rose from his seat and quickly shook his hand and nodded at him and sat back down again. Everyone was watching them keenly and there was silence and perhaps also a tension. Max was in the front of the room, and it was only now that Judy hugged him properly, indicating two empty spaces down to the right of Wolf which he had not previously noticed. Isaac worked his way up the side of the table towards Avram.

'My son,' Avram said to him. He stood up and put his arms out. Isaac went towards his father. Then father and son embraced each other in tears and everyone around the table was looking at them. Judy had both her hands in front of her face and her eyes were moist and full again. Ruth was staring down at the table in front of her. Nobody said anything while the two men remained locked together for a long time. Isaac was crying openly, but Wolf was surprised to see that Avram was also. They held each other tightly, as if they were wrestling with each other, swaying gently back and forth. After what felt like a few minutes Judy came over and embraced both of them and the three of them then separated slightly. Isaac turned and beckoned to Max, who was still standing at the front of the room, and Max came up and Avram hugged him also and the three men remained huddled like that in a small group, like figures on a stage, floodlit, or in a painted medieval scene of grief.

From his father-in-law Avram's perspective, Wolf was only the second great disaster to have occurred to his family. The first was Isaac being gay, which by all accounts had been obvious from a young age. Avram's initial approach was not subtle, apparently. He encouraged, even forced, Isaac into sports, football, hockey, he even brought him down to the local boxing club. None of these lasted long, and looking at him now, locked in an embrace with Isaac and his partner Max, the old man had clearly made his peace with the situation. This was one of the things Wolf had always found most impressive about the Jewish religion, certainly the conservative and reform branches – maybe not the Orthodox, where homosexuality was on a par with leprosy – that they weren't squeamish in any way about gay issues, or sex in general, lacking the hang-ups of Catholics. One of Wolf's Dublin school friends had come out at the age of fifty, having been with his husband, whom he had married in Canada, for almost twenty years. Wolf had heard that what upset the friend's mother most was the certain knowledge that Peter at the pearly gates would not now be letting her son through and that he would instead be condemned to the fires of hell. At the time Wolf had laughed at this aspect of the woman's misery, but part of him also envied her supernaturalist viewpoint, the vivid colouring it must have given to the world, as if there was constantly, beneath the surface of things, a movie taking place on an enormous scale, not visible to the likes of him, full of special effects and wonder. In comparison, his own godlessness seemed like a dull place, a hopeless Siberia where your life is one trumped-up charge after another. You scrabble around in it looking for bits of joy, or at least distraction. But even Avram – warrior of the Sinai, borderline racist (when it came to Arabs of any persuasion) – had come to terms with Isaac's sexuality. Wolf had heard him express acceptance of it, even if his acceptance was Job-like, as if Isaac – just like that other, biblical, Isaac – was a test that God the trickster had set him.

Isaac leaned over and gave a final kiss to his father on the cheek. Then Avram sat down and Isaac, Max and Judy took their seats.

'My God,' Isaac said after sitting next to Max, down to Wolf's right, his voice still raw with emotion, 'this is like the first RH I've made it to in forever.'

Judy placed two bowls in front of him and Max.

'Are these matzo balls gluten-free, Judy?' Isaac asked.

'Actually Allen made them.'

Allen coughed.

'This year I made them all gluten-free,' he announced. 'For those who are merely sensitive rather than outright intolerant.'

Wolf laughed, but he was the only one who did and Isaac glared at him. He got a quick glimpse of Ruth though, who looked down. She would have found it funny.

'It's your birthday soon, isn't it?' the woman across from Wolf was asking Judy. Who was she again? He looked at her, with her blue and white woollen skullcap, which frankly looked in need of a good dry clean. She could have been anybody.

'I remember it was always the week before Miriam's,' she said, 'and my own mother's, rest in peace.'

'Yes. Allen got me an appointment to see an allergist.'

'How romantic.'

'It was supposed to be a surprise, but I have this rash that keeps flaring up.'

The woman nodded and they both sat in thoughtful silence for a moment. The atmosphere around the table was subdued, as if the emotion of the previous few minutes had exhausted everyone.

'How long are you back for, Isaac?' Judy said then. Isaac

paused slightly and then said, 'I'll be able this year to ask forgiveness of you all in person, instead of via email like usual. I should set up a booth and have you all stop by on appointment!'

It was only then that he answered Judy's question. Wolf recognized this deferred response as a trait he shared with Miriam.

'We're going upstate to some friends,' he said. 'We'll be back though for Yom Kippur.'

'Friend!' Avram shouted from the head of the table. 'What friend?!'

Everyone laughed.

'Ah, I had almost forgotten about that old Israeli charm,' Isaac said. 'I guess I've been living too long amongst the sophisticates of Europe.'

He went on to say, 'It really is fabulous to be home though,' before finally addressing Avram's question, and again Wolf was reminded of Miriam. It used to irritate him no end.

'It's friends of Max's. Well, ours really, by this stage... Max worked with Helen years ago and they totally adopted him.'

'Is she Jewish?' both Avram and the woman in the skull-cap asked at the same time.

'Oh, I remember her,' Judy said, and then, looking at Max, 'She was the publisher person. At your fortieth.'

'Yes,' said Max, the first word he had spoken since arriving.

'We'll have plenty of time to discuss all this... we're not

going back to Barcelona until the twenty-fifth.' He pronounced Barcelona self-consciously, labouring the second syllable like a native Spaniard. Wolf noticed Judy smile.

'We'll be back for Yom Kippur and Mir's ceremony,' Isaac said. 'Tuesday right? Her birthday.'

An awkward silence fell over the table. Wolf had the sense that people were waiting for him to say something, but he just sat there looking back at them, at a complete loss. What was it now? He'd zoned out for a little, perhaps it was the wine. It came as a relief when Ruth spoke up from her end of the table.

'Yes,' she said, firm and confident. 'Tuesday. It is her birthday then. Or was, anyway.'

3

REALLY IT COULD have been any Starbucks in the world. He didn't know how long he'd been sitting there, but he wasn't anxious about it, in fact it was pleasant to be there. He felt that buoyancy again, listening to the music, watching those around him. A woman coming out of the ladies caught his eye. He paid her more attention the closer she came to him. When she was just a few feet from him he noticed the other coffee cup on his table. It was half-full, lipstick marks around the mouth of it. The woman sat down in front of him without saying anything. She didn't look at him, her gaze fixed on a spot on the ground. He wasn't sure whether he should say something. Perhaps she wasn't well. After some time she spoke, still looking at the ground.

'The other thing I keep thinking about is your stuff.'

Finally she looked up at him.

'What is it?' she said. 'You're looking at me like I've lost my mind.'

'Sorry,' he said, and she shook her head. She took up her coffee and drank from it, before speaking again.

'But I mean how fucked up is that, right?'

She saw that he wasn't quite following.

'Your stuff in the hotel room. In Prague,' she said. 'The

guilt I had over that, just leaving it all there. Did they ever send it on to you?'

All he could do was look back at her without answering.

The woman shook her head and looked away. Her tone changed.

'What time are you meeting Ruth anyway?'

It was the voice he recognized more than anything else. But that only increased his sense of confusion.

'I don't know.'

The woman took up her coffee.

'I thought you were an autograph hunter by the way. The other night, when you turned up in the alleyway after the show. I get them now you know.'

She laughed and then he laughed, but probably too much. She gave him a strange look. Then her tone changed back again.

'You want to hear something else hilarious? About Prague?'

She shifted around in her seat so that she was directly facing him.

He nodded.

'I actually thought you were going to propose to me,' she said. 'Not properly, I mean, I knew you were still legally married to Miriam and all, but, I don't know . . . it was stupid, a fucking promise ring or something, like what kids do. But I was convinced there was some grand gesture you were going to make that weekend. In a way you did, of course. That's always the worst thing about getting dumped, isn't it? You feel like such a moron afterwards.'

He started to say something, but god knows what. In any case, she stopped him, she hadn't got it all out of her system yet.

'I fucked our waiter. Do you remember him? The kid who flirted with me on the first night and who irritated the hell out of you. The one in that bar next to the hotel that we ended up in after dinner? Yeah, I fucked him...How pathetic, right? How low can you go? He was too polite to say no. I must have scared the shit out of him. Who is this demented crying woman? he must have thought. How low, right?'

And now she was looking at him full on.

'That was the lowest though,' she said. 'Meaning that actually it's all been pretty good since then.'

She started laughing.

'Once I got away from you, things – everything really – improved!'

She turned away from him and relaxed back in the seat, taking her coffee and drinking from it. Then she noticed something at the door and her expression changed and she sat up a little. He turned to where she was looking. Ruth was there. That was his daughter. Obviously he knew that, he recognized her straight away. Ruth had also seen them, but she stood for a second before coming over. He didn't say anything to introduce them, but that didn't seem awkward.

'Hello,' the woman said to Ruth, putting out her hand and introducing herself. Ruth paused slightly before shaking it.

'How are you settling into New York?'

'We're only visiting,' Ruth said.

'Yes, of course.'

There was an obvious silence before the woman spoke again.

'Anyway,' she said, standing up. 'I'd better get going.' She drank the rest of her coffee. Wolf stood up.

'Bring Ruth to the show now that you're here. Just call and I'll have tickets left at the door.'

They embraced and she shook hands with Ruth and said it was great to meet her in person. After she had gone Ruth went to the counter to get a coffee and Wolf was left to sit once more in the sunlight coming through the window, to soak up the restful atmosphere, the bland feel-good music. It could have been any Starbucks in the world. There was a new one not far from their house. Miriam went to it practically every day, she was totally addicted to it, though sometimes she sent him out to it on her behalf. He was always confused by her order, not just in recent times. It seemed to get more elaborate every time. Soy milk. Matcha or fracha or something. But the soy was the most important thing, he had to be sure to really emphasize it. He saw the empty cup on the table in front of him, lipstick on the rim. She must be in the ladies. He wasn't sure what was on the agenda later. Did she have a class, or perhaps there was something at her synagogue? She'd been going to it more and more in recent months. Perhaps he could talk her out of it. There was a restaurant nearby. He liked it more than she did, meaning that the ambience was better than the food. But perhaps he could get her to go with him. He looked up to see where she was. She must be at the counter. It was a surprise when Ruth appeared in front of him, an enormous coffee cup in her hand. She took the other coffee cup that was on the table, Miriam's cup, and put it in the bin, then came back and took the seat opposite him. She was staring hard at him, fierce.

'I know who she is, Mike,' she said. 'Just in case you think that I don't.'

4

ALLEN AND JUDY were waiting for them in the lobby of the hotel. Evidently they had been there a while. As soon as Wolf and Ruth appeared through the revolving doors they jumped up from the long couch by the window.

'Finally we can go already,' Judy said with exaggerated but also real exasperation. He and Ruth stood looking at them.

'Where are we going?' Wolf asked.

Now it was Judy's turn to be confused.

'What do you mean? It's like we arranged on the phone the other night. Wolfgang, we must have literally spoken for half an hour about this.'

She saw the empty face looking back at her and let out another exaggerated sigh.

'We're taking your gorgeous daughter here to MOMA and you're going off with Allen to talk about whatever it is you wanted to talk about.'

Ruth was staring at him.

'Come on, sweets,' Judy said, taking Ruth by the arm. 'Your cousins are there already. They've probably had five espressos by now. We'll have to scrape them off the walls.'

Ruth looked at Wolf as she walked out of the lobby and he could tell that she didn't want to go. He didn't want her to go either. But there was no combination of words coming to him quick enough that would change things. He simply looked back at her as she disappeared through the automatic doors, until he was looking at the empty space left behind. The light was streaming in through the thin blind of the main window, particulate matter and dust visibly swirling in it. He focused on it for a few moments. It was like a small weather system, a perfectly contained universe in miniature.

As they waited for the elevator neither Allen nor Wolf spoke, and they stood listening to the lobby music. Allen was irritating Wolf immensely. He kept hopping from one foot to the other. Could he not stand still for Christ's sake? He was like one of those things. Wolf put his hand up to his face so he didn't have to look at him. Eventually the door opened and they got in. Allen looked at Wolf, waiting for him to do something.

'I presume we're going here?' Allen said then, his finger hovering over the button that said Bar/Restaurant. Wolf didn't say anything and Allen pressed it, but nothing happened.

'Oh,' he said. 'It's probably one of those where you have to insert your key.'

He laughed, seeing Wolf's confusion.

'Your room key, Wolfgang!'

'I know that.'

Wolf found something in his back pocket and held it out in front of him. None of this made any sense. Allen took it and inserted it into the slot, then gave it back to him. He pressed the button again and they began to move. Wolf leaned against the walls, exhausted. Anything vaguely technical seemed to take a lot out of him. The elevator stopped once, but when the door opened nobody got in. Eventually they emerged on the top floor, stepping out onto thick dark carpet. Their pace slowed, both of them savouring the luxurious thickness of it.

'Makes me want to take off my shoes,' Allen said, again laughing nervously. Wolf ignored him.

A sign in front of the restaurant told them to wait for the hostess. The place was busy, with a loud din of noise coming mostly from all the way over at the far outdoor area. The hostess came, and to Wolf's surprise recognized him by name.

'I believe I have the same table for you as before,' she said.

'Oooh,' Allen said. 'A regular, if you will. I'm impressed, Wolfgang.'

Wolf felt himself tensing up with irritation.

The hostess reached under the stand and took out two menus. She brought the men across the dark interior of the restaurant to the outdoor area and seated them. The air was already a relief. They were exactly at the point between indoors and outdoors, the demarcation line running under Wolf's feet. He ordered a Scotch before the hostess dissappeared. The table right next to them was rowdy, two middle-aged men shouting in what sounded like Russian accompanied by much younger, very attractive women with the appearance of models. The men were drinking shots and more or less ignoring the women.

'So . . .' Allen said, but he left it at that, and they sat for a while looking around them.

Thankfully a waitress was quick to appear with Wolf's drink. The feel of the cool glass improved his mood instantly. He sipped from it, continuing to look around. It was a warm day, just after noon. New York could be heard over the wall and the breeze which carried tiny pieces of grit in it, as if the sun was laced with it. He regretted not having his sunglasses with him. He could feel the air conditioning from indoors on his right-hand side. A couple of tables down, a young boy was playing with a balloon. Other diners batted it back to him with irritation when it floated their way. The boy thought it was a game. His mother was looking down at her phone.

'Is everything OK, Wolfgang?'

He had almost forgotten Allen was there. The earnest face and thick beard now looking back at him. Allen was wearing a shirt and tie, a jacket, all of which seemed decades old but still in reasonable condition. Wolf had a small burst of curiosity about him, this cousin of his sitting across from him. Or cousin-in-law, whatever he was to him, a sort-of relation.

'I mean, no offence, but you seem agitated.'

Wolf took up more of his drink. He maintained eye contact, almost in the form of a challenge, but it was a pretty empty one. For a brief glorious few seconds he allowed himself to know absolutely nothing, who he was or where, what his role was supposed to be, nothing. He grinned like an idiot. The sun and the warm breeze, the booze which was already beginning to take effect, it was like magic, he didn't care about anything. The little boy's balloon came towards him, a tiny meteor meant only for his head. That seemed right somehow. A waiter reached out and batted it back.

'How's Ruth, Wolfgang?'

Allen was staring at him again. The earnest eye contact. Why was he bringing up Ruth? That was his daughter. He wondered where she was, he hadn't seen her in a while.

'Fine. Why?'

'Yes, she does seem mostly fine. What a tough time it's been for her.'

He paused, gave a little cough, before continuing.

'And she seems to be eating well, at least when she's at our house. Normal, I would have described it as. For a teenager anyway. But I suppose that's the sort of thing we have to keep an eye on ... I'm speaking from ignorance here, but I'd imagine these disorders can flare up at times like this. What's it been now, two years since she was in the hospital?'

Wolf must have given him a dubious look.

'No, no, you're right,' Allen said. 'More like three or even four. But they're serious things. A friend's daughter had something similar. But she's totally fine now. Anyway, listen to me, rambling on. I guess I wanted you to know that Judy and I are here. For both of you. Whatever is going on with her.'

Wolf just sat there. He allowed the silence to gather, the surrounding noise to reassert itself. Allen sat back in his chair.

'What do you mean *whatever is going on with her*?'

He didn't intend the tone of his voice to be so aggressive.

'Nothing. Nothing!' Allen said. 'I mean, it's just clear that she's having a tough time. I'm positive it's all perfectly normal. That whole thing with Josh for instance, I think they just rub each other up the wrong way. They're at that age, aren't they?'

'That doesn't sound like her. That's not Miriam.'

'Ruth.'

Wolf stared back at him.

'Yes. Ruth,' he said. The name felt strange as he said it though. There was a small brief panic. That was her name, wasn't it?

A waiter came and checked on them, but they both ignored him. Wolf had lost his sense of ease, that buoyancy. He was aware that he wasn't quite following things, but at the same time he wasn't too bad. Mainly he was just tired, worn out, and also impatient. I mean, if this person had something to say why didn't he just spit it out? Again he felt a spasm of irritation, even anger, at this man sitting across from him who seemed so well informed about things. This was his first time hearing about any disorder or illness affecting Ruth. Where was she anyway? He hadn't seen her in a while. Ruth. Again the name felt strange to him. Allen was waiting for him to say something.

'What *thing with Josh*?'

Allen put both hands on the table, splaying out his fingers.

'Oh you remember. It was no big deal. The trip to the World Trade Center memorial? I think it was the first couple of days you guys got here. Josh can be very argumentative. He's going through that whole left-wing über-liberal phase at the moment. He's big into the whole BDC boycott thing.

I guess we didn't realise Ruth was so political also. You know, that T-shirt she was wearing. *I stand with Israel.*'

Wolf stared back at him. The last time he had been to the World Trade Center there were two enormous towers coming out of the ground, the biggest things he'd ever seen.

'Like I say,' Allen continued, 'it's all perfectly normal. Frankly it was good to see her come out of her shell a little.'

He paused. They were interrupted by the waiter, who placed a beer down in front of Allen. Wolf didn't recall him ordering it.

Allen admired the beer for a second then seemed to really enjoy the drink he took from it. He used the sleeve of his jacket to rub across his mouth.

'Boy, that's good,' he said. Then his tone changed a little and he leaned forward.

'I would be careful of that friend of hers though if I were you. The one she met in Israel. Ingrit? She picked up Ruth at the house a couple of times. She's attached to the Chabad House in our neighbourhood. Ruth's been spending a lot of time there. In fact, when she stays with us we barely see her. That's what they do, you know. They lure you in with meals and wine and prayers, create that sense of community. They're good at it. They'll do anything to get an influx of young blood. If you're not careful they'll have Ruth married off to some yeshiva student!'

A loud bang caused both of them to look around. It came from the next table. One of the Russians was holding his steak knife in the air. He'd used the tip of it to burst the boy's balloon that must have floated in their direction. The young lad stood in front of the grinning man, too stunned to cry. When he turned around Wolf recognized his pained expression, how helpless he looked, and both he and Allen watched as the little boy trudged off. One of the women followed him and put some notes of cash into his hand, rubbed the top of his head, and said something to the boy's mother, who had finally looked up from her phone.

When Allen turned back it was Wolf's turn to be staring at him.

'Can she come and live with you?'

Allen didn't say anything.

'Ruth,' Wolf said. Again, his daughter's name was strange when he spoke it out loud. 'Can she come and live with you?'

It was as if Allen didn't understand the question.

'I mean, assuming money is not an issue,' Wolf said. 'Let's put that to one side for the moment. But if I asked you to, would you look after her for me? Allow her to come and live in your house?'

Allen looked back at him. A few seconds went by which seemed longer than that, the two men staring at each other.

'Why, where are you going?'

Wolf gave a little laugh then took up his drink but put it down again.

'No, no, it's not that,' he said. 'I wish,' and he laughed.

He sat forward in his chair.

'I've got dementia, Allen. The early stages of it.'

He gave another little laugh. Allen was staring at him. The

earnest expression was now something else. Wolf had a small rush of affection for him.

He started to say something else but stopped and just sat looking openly at Allen. The sounds around them seemed to intensify and abate. He was suddenly aware of the altitude they were sitting at, projected into the sky as they were, the air currents swirling around them.

'Wolfgang, you're going to have to explain this.'

Wolf laughed. Something about Allen's manner. He felt like he had the clearest picture of him. Probably Allen had never done a bad thing in his life, couldn't even conceive of it. He and his wife had one of those marriages where both parties would survive into old age, adopting each other's habits, then die within days of each other. Miriam had deserved one of those. She had the temperament for it. She just happened to choose poorly. Judy. That was the wife's name. Judy and Allen, he of the bearded, earnest face looking back at him, waiting for him to say something. With bated breath. Isn't that what they say? Bated. Perhaps not, it didn't sound right either. The waitress came to the table next to them, not the Russians', but that of a couple Wolf was just noticing now for the first time. He allowed his attention to linger on them. He knew that Allen was still looking at him, taking everything in, horrified at what Wolf had just told him, going through the ramifications. Possibly one or two of the other tables had been listening to them, although not this young happy couple who were hearing about the specials from the waitress. As far as he could make out, neither of them were married. He took up his drink. It was such a gorgeous day. The sun didn't seem to be so laced with grit now. He allowed himself to have that feeling again, of not caring, not knowing anything, that incredible buoyancy. There were times when he could summon this feeling at will, and that ability seemed to be increasing in frequency. It was perhaps the sole consolation. He turned back to his cousin-in-law, or whatever the bearded, earnest man across from him was. He smiled at him. Allen. That was his name. Allen.

'About six months ago,' he said, 'maybe more, I started to become forgetful. Not a big deal, really. Not being able to make my way home. But from the supermarket, that I'd been to a thousand times. I knew something was up.'

He stopped. He was telling a story. He knew that he was liable to say anything. It felt good.

'Miriam noticed things, stupid things, leaving my bloody phone in the fridge, finding the front door of the house wide open . . .'

He wasn't sure if these things had happened to him or to someone else. The phone. He thought he could even remember Miriam coming across it. He had an image of her holding it up between her thumb and index finger, as if it stank, a strange look on her face. Perhaps he was inventing all this. It felt right though. Allen was looking at him, hanging on his every word. He'd better continue with the story, no matter how reliable it might or might not be.

'There were lots of other things too. Poor concentration. Lapses.' Again, he presumed all this to be true.

'Nothing major. I probably would have ignored it, to be

honest. If it wasn't for the family history. My mother. She had the same thing, you see.'

He paused and briefly closed his eyes. Allen didn't say anything. His concentration level almost had a noise to it. His lips were tense.

'Miriam pointed out that I didn't drive any more. I didn't tell her that the very idea of getting into a car fucking terrified me. I stayed close to home, and if I did have to go anywhere I would order a car service. I had these cards printed with my address on them and would hand them to the driver. I also wrote everything down.'

That part at least was definitely true, verifiable. He picked up his notebook which was on the table beside him.

'This is my memory now.'

He could have gone on and on. It wasn't just the absences, the gaps he could speak of, those he was aware of anyway, and which seemed to come out of nowhere, like rents in the fabric of things, spread out in front of him like a great high depth that had suddenly emerged beneath him. There were also the physical symptoms that were no doubt part of things, the body perhaps realizing that there was some fault in the centre of itself, a flaw in the programming. The thin breathing, the chest bones that seemed to be lighter, flimsier. The familiar faces which he saw everywhere like ghosts, they appeared out of place and also out of time; an old teacher from his childhood, a school friend, his father, they would materialize on the street in front of him and so vividly that he felt like reaching out his hand towards them, a perfect stranger, who was then gone. Or alternatively a face would mean nothing to him, even though it was obvious from the way they were talking that they had met before, the mother of one of Ruth's friends, her teacher, a neighbour.

'Anyway,' he continued, 'I went to my GP. She referred me to a memory specialist, a new one on me. The memory guy did an MRI scan and something called a PET scan. To cut a long story short, it's what they call early Alzheimer's. Not full blown yet, but not reversible all the same.'

He took up his drink. They sat in silence then for a while. There was a weight to Allen's silence, you could virtually hear his mind cranking through its gears, absorbing everything.

'Miriam never told us.'

'She didn't know. I didn't want to worry her, given her illness.'

'Look, it's mostly fine,' he said, seeing Allen's face, which seemed to go up a register in its horror. 'I mean, really, apart from those occasional inconveniences. Moments of blank as I call them. And this doesn't help of course,' he said, holding up his drink and shaking it a little. Allen was still looking at him in horror. It made Wolf want to try and reassure him.

'But I really don't have it too bad yet,' he said. 'Like I say, it's in the relatively early stages. The doctors can give only very rough estimates about the course of things, how it will go and when. I could be mostly normal for a little while yet, you never know.'

He stopped talking. Allen still didn't say anything and Wolf couldn't make out his face. The sun had changed its position in the sky and Wolf was getting the full brunt of it. He could have moved his face slightly to the left, but he just left it hanging there to burn. To their left another commotion broke out as the Russians got up to go, struggling to their feet, leaning on each other and being helped up by their female companions, to the men's great hilarity. A glass fell to the floor. A wad of cash lay on the table, open to the breeze. One of the women tried to gather the notes and place them under a plate, which of course the men also found hilarious. One of them took out his wallet and threw another few bills onto the table, and they also blew away. The waitress hurried over to help and the two men walked off, a little unsteady on their feet. As they were going by, one of the men put his hands on Wolf's shoulders.

'Ah, my English friend,' he said, laughing, his voice coming from directly over Wolf's head, his entire weight bearing down on him.

He spoke to Allen.

'You know, I paid ten thousand pounds for one of his pictures. A photograph. Can you believe it?' The man mimicked taking a photo. 'Snap!' he said, laughing.

He patted Wolf on the back again.

'Tell me. How is your beautiful daughter?' he said. 'You must say to her not to take my friend so seriously, OK? We men like to joke around, but yeah yeah, perhaps too much, I admit it.'

Then he was distracted by one of the passing busboys.

'WAITER. Come here please...I want to pay for my friend here.'

He pushed a fistful of cash into the hands of the bemused

young man, who appeared not to understand English. The other Russian was already in the main part of the restaurant shouting back at his companion.

'My friend is eager for Thai massage,' the man said, before pressing down hard on Wolf's shoulders and giving them another squeeze. Then he was gone.

Allen was looking at Wolf, incredulous. They watched as the Russian made his way unsteadily through the restaurant.

'For example,' Wolf said, 'I don't remember meeting him.'

Allen's eyes seemed to widen a little. He was about to say something but stopped and the two of them sat for a moment watching the busboys tidy up the mess beside them. When Allen turned around Wolf was ready for him, all business, on the table in front of him his open notebook, which he was able to use as a reference.

'I've opened a bank account here for Ruth. It's got over eight hundred thousand in it. Dollars. The account is in her name, but I also want to put it in Judy's, I'll have to have her sign a form. That should more than cover things until she's eighteen, high school fees, food and board, clothes. There's also a trust fund that she can access when she's eighteen. There's over six hundred thousand in it. Sterling. My solicitor in London is looking after it, but I would like to make you and Judy executors. There's also property, back in London, our house in Islington. We're not going back to it, which incidentally Ruth doesn't know yet. The deeds of title are now in Ruth's name, but the market's shit so the best thing for now is to keep it rented. A management company has taken it on. You won't have to worry about it. If for some reason it does become a hassle just sell it. Maurice will take care of everything.'

Allen stared back at him.

'There's something missing in all this,' Allen said finally.

Wolf stared at him, unsure what he meant.

'You,' Allen said. 'You're speaking like you won't be around. Or am I imagining that?'

Wolf smiled at Allen. He felt enormous goodwill towards him. To his astonishment, his eyes stung a little and there was a real danger, with the sun, the booze, that they could even stray into sentimentality. It came as a relief when the waitress came over to check on them.

'But no,' Wolf said, after she had gone and the moment of weakness had passed. He looked directly at Allen.

'You're not imagining it,' he said.

5

HE WALKED DOWN Second Avenue in the direction of the East Village, through that nondescript part of Manhattan below Gramercy which he had always found virtually characterless, past its storefronts, chains, bodegas, bars, a general zone of disenchantment. He came to St Marks Place and remembered that he had got married there. Maybe that was the reason he'd headed there in the first place. He had nothing to do for the rest of the day. Ruth was apparently going back to Brooklyn with them all. He was aimless and walked slowly. It was surprising how little St Marks had changed. The same shabby five- or six-storeyed buildings of different muted tones, the fire escapes hanging down in front of them, boxing them in, dead trees sprouting up out of the broken pavement. One building was a ruin, gutted by fire and draped with dead vines, thick ropes of a pure black ivy. A modern high-end development beside it stuck out, perched like a new species of bird, recently introduced, sleek and vicious, disdainful of its surroundings. St Cyril's he remembered, the Theatre 80 venue further on and a few other familiar buildings, but none of the stores or restaurants were the same. The Yaffa Cafe was gone, for instance, one of Miriam's haunts, and the corner bar next to it that used to heave at all hours of the day and night. Now it was some clothing chain. The absence of these certain landmarks seemed to him a faltering in the collective memory rather than his own; for once, he was the one with the unblemished recollection.

He continued eastward, the sidewalk crowded with week-enders, tourists, entire families strolling. The racial demographic was mostly Asian. An enormous sushi bar had taken over one of the buildings halfway down the block, its bottom two floors opened out, the basement sunk into the ground; brightly lit, without a single shadow in the whole structure. Its size and brightness and noise dominated the street, every inch of its floor covered by customers clinging to the building's surface, their din constant like a density of seabirds. An unreasonable panic rose up in his chest. He couldn't find the site of his wedding. Maybe it had never happened, none of it. He went on, paying less attention to his surroundings. He couldn't decide whether everything had changed or nothing had. It was exhausting. He found himself in Tompkins Square Park. The open space gave some relief, and he did a lap of it. There was a festival-like atmosphere, not threatening at all, hordes of the young scattered around the benches, sitting on the grass, dressed the same as one another, several with guitars, skateboarders doing tricks, not an elderly person to be seen for miles around. A man on one of the benches was entirely covered by pigeons – he had birdseed in his upturned palms and stuffed into his shirt pocket and spread about his person in the folds of his clothing and on his lap, and he sat there statue-like, arms spread out, the pigeons descending in their droves and covering him in a fur. People stared in disgust, giving him a wide berth; the smell was bad, rats with wings somebody said. He walked back across Avenue A onto St Marks, and there it was, the old apartment building where he and Miriam had married. What a relief to find it, it was next to the large sushi place. He stood in front of it and tried to summon the depth of feeling and memory that he knew was in there somewhere. A group of people walking behind him laughed and joked. He looked at them and their faces froze into grins. He remained in front of the building for a long time. It hadn't changed. It had the same dilapidated appearance, off-white, with rubbish in the small front yard. The ceremony had taken place on the upper floor, presided over by one of Miriam's friends. The building was in darkness and it did not look at all like the sort of place such an event could happen in. There was a small roof deck which gave you views of the skyline; when you stood on it you felt you had been elevated right into the centre of that firmament. He stood and waited, but nothing happened apart from the continuous stream of people walking behind him on the pavement and the din of the place next door and the even louder silence of the place in front of him. The past was five minutes ago and it was fifty years ago and it was an eternity. It was locked away inside this building or it had never happened or had yet to happen; the memories were living dead things, like people kept prisoner, going through their motions, unable to leave. Miriam was in there somewhere, if he only knew how to look for her.

The noise was his phone ringing. It took him a moment to locate it in the pocket.

'Where are you?'

He held the phone to his ear but said nothing, like an infant.

'WHERE ARE YOU?'

Still he said nothing.

'It was you who wanted to talk, Wolfgang,' the voice said then. 'Well we're here, waiting for you.'

Wolf asked him where and there was a loud sigh like he'd been told a hundred times already.

'I'll text you the address. Just get in a fucking cab already.'

6

ISAAC WAS SITTING at the bar of Mandianos on West
10th, leaning back on a high leather-backed stool. Beside
him was his friend Sophie Appleton, the pop star, who Wolf
recognized straight away. He even remembered the last time
he had seen her, looking out at him from a news stand at
some unspecified point in time, perhaps recently, dressed in
sombre black. In the picture she was being led out of a church
in England, her distinctive enormous sunglasses covering her
eyes. SOPHIE'S DAD DEAD, the headline shouted.

Isaac turned to look at him as he came through the door
but didn't react or say anything. Wolf went over and stood
behind them.

'Soph,' Isaac said without turning, 'you know Wolfgang,
right? My *brother*-in-law?'

Isaac was drunk, or well on his way, which generally didn't
take much. In front of him was a champagne glass containing some sort of cocktail.

Sophie turned around. She was laughing at something
and put her hand on Wolf's arm.

'I'm sorry,' she said. 'Isaac's been telling me about his
career plans.'

'They're not plans Sophie!' Isaac said. 'They're aspirations!'

'Sorry, aspirations.'

Sophie turned to Wolf.

'He wants to start a foundation. I told him he should maybe start by getting a job first.'

She had the same drink in front of her as Isaac.

'I just want to try and help people, you know?' Isaac said. 'So fucking shoot me.'

Wolf pulled out the stool to Isaac's left and sat up on it. Nobody else was at the bar. In fact, the entire restaurant was empty. Perhaps they had opened it specially for Sophie. The bartender put down a menu and a small paper drink mat. Wolf told him he would try whatever they were drinking.

'We're celebrating,' Isaac said, and then he lowered his voice to virtually a whisper. 'Soph just found out she's doing the Super Bowl next year ... But you can't tell anyone, it's a total secret!' He put his index finger over his lips, a gesture Wolf hadn't seen anyone make in years, perhaps since childhood.

'I don't care,' Sophie said. 'You can tell whoever. I don't give a shit.'

'No, Sophie!' Isaac said, jumping around on his stool to face her. 'It hasn't been announced officially yet! You'll get in trouble with the corporates!'

'Don't be dramatic. They don't give a shit either.'

'Well, in any case you don't have to worry,' said Isaac. 'Wolf is great at keeping secrets. Isn't that right ,Wolf?'

'Just don't fucking tweet it or anything,' Sophie said.

She lifted her glass to her mouth and sipped barely anything from it.

Her strong cockney accent came as a surprise to Wolf. He had always associated her with New York. He'd forgotten, or maybe never knew in the first place, that she was from London. The barman made some finishing touches to his drink, then placed it down in front of him. He admired the swirl of colour in it for a second, then said cheers and raised his drink to Isaac and Sophie. They returned the gesture. Isaac's glass was empty. He asked for another one. Wolf could sense Sophie looking at him. She leaned across Isaac.

'I feel like I knew Miriam quite well. She was a really cool person ...'

Isaac's body stiffened. He sat back in his chair, very upright, his eyes closed. Sophie looked up at him, irritated. Isaac opened his eyes and his demeanour just as quickly changed back again.

'Yeah, remember that time in Barcelona?' he said.

Sophie sat back, still looking at Wolf. There was more she wanted to say.

'With Max's friends?' Isaac continued. 'When Mir came to visit? Soph?'

'Yes, Isaac,' Sophie said, breaking off eye contact with Wolf. 'I remember.'

'We must have stayed up for like two whole nights partying ...' Isaac said.

'Where was Ruth?' Wolf asked, cutting him off. This was the first he had heard about any Barcelona trip.

'What?' Isaac said. 'We took her with us of course. Noah was there as well, so there were plenty of people looking out for her. Ruth was always very close to Noah ...'

'Who's Noah?' Wolf said.

Isaac stared at him for a second.

'OK, OK, I exaggerate! Ruth wasn't up the two full nights ... But in Catalonia it's like totally normal for the kids to stay up late, to eat with the adults ...'

'She was fine,' Sophie said, leaning in front of Isaac again. 'Don't mind him, it was actually quite tame. There were other kids around, even younger than Ruth. My brother was there with his wife and their twins. We had like two nannies.'

'Hey, don't ruin my story,' Isaac said in mock anger, but with a trace of the real thing.

They all reached for their drinks and then none of them spoke. Wolf sat perfectly still. Noah. Barcelona. He had a hundred questions, but everything about his own body, the thin breaths it was taking, the choking sensation in the throat, the racing heart, told him to sit as still as possible, that it would be better that way. A clench of rage and frustration came over him. Nobody noticed anything and he took one deep breath and held it. He stood to take off his jacket. It gave him a chance to calm down.

Isaac asked the barman to see a food menu. He had to ask twice as the barman was absorbed in the book he was reading. From the cover it seemed like a cheap romantic novel, which was a little incongruous, given the barman's physicality and rough, tattooed appearance. Sophie must have had the same thought because she made eye contact with Wolf and smiled.

'So what did you want to talk about?' Isaac said.

Wolf looked back at him.

'You said that it was something important.'

Sophie stepped off her stool and excused herself.

'You can stay, Soph.'

'Don't be a dick, Isaac,' she said, and walked off in the direction of the toilets. Wolf finished the rest of his drink and asked the bartender for a Scotch. He sensed Isaac's impatience and he was tempted to make more of it, to draw things out.

'I probably just wanted to let you know that Ruth will be moving to New York.'

'Probably?' Isaac said.

'She'll be staying with Judy and Allen.'

Isaac didn't say anything. The bartender put Wolf's drink down in front of him.

'I figured it would be best for her here,' he said.

'Right,' said Isaac. 'To have some *family* around her.'

Wolf ignored him. Isaac was uncharacteristically quiet then, mulling things over.

'Do me a favour and don't speak about it yet though,' Wolf said. 'There are some details . . . Also, Ruth doesn't know yet.'

'She doesn't know!'

'I wanted everyone else to know first. In case there were unforeseen issues that I hadn't thought of.'

Isaac seemed to accept this and left it at that. Neither of them said anything. After a while Isaac leaned forward and picked up the menu and it was as if nothing had been said. The restaurant was so quiet he could hear the noise of the hand dryer from the ladies and a few seconds later the door opened and Sophie returned, her thick heels making a loud noise across the floor. Isaac asked the bartender about the menu. He wanted to know if the pasta salad could be made gluten-free and if there were any walnuts in it. Also, was it low or high sodium content. Sophie glanced at Wolf as she got up on her stool, giving her head the slightest shake. He smiled. Isaac concentrated on the menu a final time and then ordered something.

'I hope Ruth's doing OK?' Sophie said to Wolf, breaking the silence that had descended on them. 'She and Miriam were so close, Ruth was like a mini-Miriam that time I was with them, she seemed to be taking right after her . . .'

'Thankfully,' Isaac said.

'Sweet kid,' Sophie said. 'Did you bring her up Jewish?'

Wolf turned to face her. Her glasses made her face a mask.

'Like did you guys do the whole bat mitzvah thing?'

He was about to say no when Isaac jumped in.

'Yes, of course. That was very important to Mir. Me and Max flew in for it specially.'

'So did you go up to the bema, Wolfgang?' Sophie asked, and again he looked back at her, at a total loss.

'Wolf wasn't there,' Isaac said. 'He was away off with one of his girlfriends.' He laughed as if he had cracked a joke.

'Besides,' Isaac continued, 'Wolf is borderline anti-Semitic.'

'You're Jewish then?' Wolf said to Sophie, again ignoring Isaac. Her dark glasses fixed on him.

'I'm a celebrity,' she said after a delay, and the three of them laughed.

Isaac got up to go to the restroom. The bartender had also gone somewhere, so it was just Wolf and Sophie at the bar.

'We're not exactly close,' he said.

Again there was a delay before she spoke, as if she was really considering what he had said. He wondered if this was something practised, perhaps a necessity for someone in her position.

'With Isaac you're always closer than you think,' she said then. 'He virtually invented the needy state ... which, you know, coming from a diva is fucking saying something.'

He laughed. The bartender reappeared and came over to them, clearing the area a little. Both of them watched as if he was performing a skilled task. He knocked over a glass of water but then caught it without spilling a drop.

She did have a reputation as a bit of a diva. It occurred to Wolf that he actually knew quite a bit about Sophie's life. It's ridiculous what memory decides to hold fast on to. Through Miriam he had kept up to date with her career, which must qualify as a long one at this stage. She had been on the go now for what, fifteen, twenty years, ever since Juilliard, where her friendship with Isaac dated from. Wolf seemed to recall that she had left early, after her big break of appearing in one of Madonna's videos. It was hard to believe it now, but Sophie was a sort of Britney Spears type at the time, very slim, fit, what they used to call a sex symbol, with the appearance of seeming to be barely out of childhood. He knew that she had been married to an actor and there was some scandal in which he had left her. The guy went on to win an Oscar. She had problems with her weight. Drug issues, rehab, et cetera, he was surprised to see her drinking alcohol. Then in more recent times she had had a comeback of sorts and had become something of a gay icon.

'I've seen your work,' she said to him.

Wolf stared back at her. The sunglasses. The earnestness in her voice. He laughed, genuinely, the fact that he had no earthly idea what she was talking about. He felt that sense of lightness again, as if he could float off if he chose to. Sophie seemed a little perplexed. In many ways she reminded him of Ruth, the slightly defensive tone of her voice, something about her presence. There was even a physical resemblance, with her dark hair, long and full, her pale complexion, and a sort of forbearance, that he knew his daughter had with other people, just not particularly with him. Certainly he was in no rush for Isaac to return, with all his angst.

Wolf leaned over towards her.

'I have to be honest,' he said. 'I have no idea what you're talking about.'

He laughed as if he had cracked a joke. Sophie looked at him.

'I mean your ECM stuff,' she said, slightly impatient. 'I've always had a bit of an obsession with Mr Eicher. Fat chance that he'd ever record me, but still, a girl can dream. I went to that exhibition you guys had a while back, all the cover art, even bought a few pieces, including one of yours by the way.'

'Ah,' he said. ECM. Manfred Eicher's record label, which Wolf's entire career had more or less been based on, or certainly the most interesting part of it. It felt like a lot of time had passed since he had thought about any of these things. It was almost as if she was talking about someone else.

'It was always a dream of mine to work with him,' Sophie said. 'Hey, next time you're talking to him put in a word for me, will ya? I could do a sort of Norma Winstone thing, I love those albums. Did you do any of her artwork at all?'

He shook his head and they sat in silence for a few moments. He presumed that Sophie wasn't being serious. She herself would be the first to admit that she didn't fit into the label's ethos, given her status as one of the most commercial acts on the planet. ECM, with its essentially puritan air, it was like a religion to some people. That minimalist northern strain which runs through everything they do, right up to and including the artwork that they use for their album covers, some of which had become iconic by now, one or two of his own pieces, as well as that of the others associated with the label – Barbara Wojirsch most notably, of course – however you want to describe it, that bleak and stark sublime sensibility, you can practically feel the wind whipping in your face, the majesty of the sky over your head which seems to contain everything, the beauty which, according to Rilke, is representative of the terror we are capable of enduring, the joy contained within the shadow of mortality. The sublime, in other words, which to Wolf for some reason always had the setting of physical harshness in its background; a privation, a barrenness, a sense of North. It had been blind luck that led to his involvement with Manfred Eicher's great project. He had been introduced to him through the Estonian composer Arvo Pärt, after being invited to attend Pärt's Lamentate concert at the Tate Modern in 2002. Thankfully it was an occasion he could recall vividly, and what a relief this realization was to him as he sat beside Sophie, both of them content in each other's silence. The Pärt concert took place beneath the sculpture Marsyas, by Anish Kapoor, assembled in the large Turbine Hall. It was truly awesome, Gulliveresque in its obscene dimensions, breathtaking. After it was over he had wandered around the hall in a sort of prolonged daze looking up at it. He really didn't know how to describe it to himself in ways that he could make sense of, how to even look at it, to get his head around it, the thing was so strange and unsettling, too big for the senses to handle, hanging there over the heads of all the people who, like him, were wandering around beneath it, stunned to silence. The sculpture – if that's even the right word for it – gave all the appearance of being a permanent fixture, as if it had always been there, pre-dating the building even, which may as well have been assembled around it, with the express purpose of protecting it, like an artefact from an ended world, somehow more ancient than the land on which it stood. On multiple occasions since he had searched for pictures of it on the internet, but none did justice to the experience. You couldn't even see it all at once, extending as it did around the corner into the other section of the enormous hall. It consisted of three metal rings, over which had been stretched some kind of raw flesh-coloured PVC, supposedly depicting the flayed body of Marsyas, and representing the price he paid in the ancient myth for challenging the god Apollo to a musical contest and having the gall to win. Apollo took him to a cave and skinned him alive, and the myth is generally interpreted as a cautionary tale for hubris. This was all explained in the programme notes, but he found the mythical allusions too abstract, somewhat forced, notwithstanding the vividness of the colour, which did in fairness bring to mind the screaming pain and agony of the skinless state; you could almost hear Marsyas's howls reverberating through the hall as he came to his excruciating end. But the entire construction represented far more than that; he struggled to specify what exactly, as he wandered under and around it both before the concert and afterwards, the music ringing in his ears. Arvo Pärt had written about the structure, which apparently was the inspiration for the Lamentate piece. This was its world premiere, recorded and released by ECM as part of Manfred Eicher's New Series. Pärt had written that it was a song of woe, a lament not for the dead but for us, the living, who have no easy time coping with the world's suffering and despair. The music left you in no doubt about the awe and terror of that final border separating time from timelessness. It was present also in the Marsyas, not so much in the sum of what your eyes saw or in any pretence of totality, but in the enormous size of the sculpture, which paradoxically seemed only to indicate what remained unseen, as in a glimpse. Or something like that, and such were the rambling and hard-to-credit thoughts that were in his head at the time and which he could remember now with perfect clarity. Like the trumpets on Judgement Day, Pärt had written, quoting Mozart. Dies irae. How men

will tremble and grow pale When Justice comes with sword
and scale To weigh the faults and sort the fates of all!

'Where the fuck is Isaac anyway?'

He had almost forgotten Sophie was sitting beside him,
how at ease he felt in her company. She was staring at him
with her big dark glasses. 'Did he disappear down the urinal
or what?'

'Maybe it's that squirrel diet of his,' Wolf said.

She looked at him.

'It's got him all bunged up,' he said.

Sophie laughed. She had a good full-throated smoker's
laugh, and sure enough she then broke into a strenuous fit of
coughing. The bartender appeared out of nowhere and put
some water in front of her. Wolf rested his hand lightly on
Sophie's back. It sounded as if she was hacking up bits of lung.

'I don't want to be responsible for a celebrity death,'
he said, patting her on the back, and she laughed and then
coughed again, but not as bad this time. The bartender refilled
her water glass and Sophie leaned over on the bar, intermit-
tently clearing her throat. He removed his hand from her
back and they sat in silence waiting for her to fully recover.

As if on cue, Isaac appeared at the door to the toilets.
They looked over at him, but he remained standing there,
looking at the floor with a wild facial expression, exaggerated like a cartoon character. For a second Wolf thought
his brother-in-law must have lost his mind, possibly taken
drugs, but then he realized he was on the phone. He had one
of those ridiculous hands-free devices attached to his ear.

'That's not what we agreed, Marco!' Isaac said. 'That is *not* what we agreed!' He stamped his foot like a little boy. A pause, and the look of shock and disbelief on his face grew even more pronounced.

'No, Marco, no. No, no, no!'

Isaac turned and went back through the toilet door, slamming it shut after him. They could still hear him from the other side of it. His voice grew distant and they heard the sound of another door opening, perhaps leading into the alleyway. It closed then and they couldn't hear him any more.

Sophie shook her head at Wolf and they both laughed. Music began to play and they looked over at the bartender, who was standing where the system was. There were a few stop-starts before he settled on something, feel-good soft rock, it sounded good actually. Wolf felt perfectly relaxed. It was something about Sophie's company, the alcohol too of course. The newspaper image of her came back to him, the same dark glasses she was wearing now, although it could have been an image from years ago, he had no idea.

'You lost your father,' he said. 'I think I saw something about it.'

Sophie looked back at him, a little surprised. She reached for her glasses on the bar and put them back on but didn't say anything.

'Was he sick for long?'

'Motor neurone disease.'

'The newspaper said you were estranged from him.'

'And they always know the truth of course.'

She stirred her drink.

'Yeah, he left my mum and me when I was young. I don't know if you ever quite get past that. But recently it's been better . . . Or had been anyway. It wasn't a good end though. I'd like to forget that part.'

The barman was back behind the bar now and Sophie asked him for 'one of those', pointing with her thumb at Wolf's Scotch. He put down a glass of ice and filled the Scotch in front of her. Sophie stared at the drink, pursing her lips, and it was as if she was back there, in whatever room her father lay wasting in. She shuddered a little and picked up her drink. He was struck again by the resemblance to Ruth. It sort of flickered in and out. He had the strong and ridiculous feeling that he was in fact speaking to his daughter, or a future version of her. It was a pleasant feeling, Ruth minus any hostility towards him. He allowed himself to go with it.

'And that earlier hurt . . .' he said. 'Does that? I mean . . .'

He stopped, unclear even to himself what he was trying to say. He felt foolish, his face was flushed, he was liable to say anything.

Sophie was looking at him with a strange smile on her mouth.

'You want to know if bad daddies recover their little girls' affections,' she said. 'That time when we adored you. When you were like a superfuckinghero coming through the door in the evening time. When all we wanted was for you to pick us up and carry us over your head. When you could literally do any fucking thing in the world.'

Her voice had a trace of anger in it, her opaque glasses fixed on him the entire time.

She smiled.

'The answer is mostly no, I'm afraid.'

He could tell the bartender was listening to them, but he didn't care. He looked straight at Sophie.

'Mostly?'

She laughed.

'Well, nothing's a hundred per cent, is it?'

Just then the front door of the restaurant opened and Isaac came striding through.

'Where have you been?' Sophie asked.

'What are you guys talking about without me?' Isaac said, ignoring her question.

Sophie gave a little frown at Wolf. Isaac came over to the bar.

'We were talking about Wolf's art, ECM n'all,' Sophie said.

'Oh, the mordancy! The mordancy!' Isaac said in a theatrical tone, but clearly in a much better mood, his difficulties sorted out with whoever Marco was. 'Just go ahead and slit my wrists!' he said, slumping over the back of his stool.

Sophie and Wolf laughed.

'Hey, does anyone want to go to Marie's Crisis?' Isaac was now standing directly behind them. 'Soph?' he said, as he came closer, his voice almost pleading.

'Sure,' she said. 'Whatever you want, Isaac.'

7

THEY MADE THEIR way across Sixth Avenue and along Christopher Street. It was getting dark and a lot of people were about. Many of them had been drinking and it felt like two in the morning even though it was well before that, not even eight o'clock yet. A hedonism was detectable in the air, an end-of-days feeling to the mood, as there always was in that part of the city. They went down the steps into Marie's Crisis. A bald man with glasses was playing piano in the pit, the area packed with gay men standing around him, singing at the top of their voices. Sophie took off her glasses, hoping it would make her less conspicuous, but was recognized almost immediately. Wolf was surprised at how she handled it. He would have put money on her switching to extroversion, but instead she seemed to shrink back into herself. At one point she even grabbed his arm and pulled him closer. She leaned against the back wall, positioning herself directly behind Isaac, who seemed to expand into the space around Sophie that people were looking at, nudging each other, pointing her out. Isaac was having the time of his life, interacting with the people standing around him, staying very close to Sophie, and singing with gusto the Broadway numbers the piano man was belting out and which the whole place was joining in on. Sophie and Wolf were the only people in the place not singing.

'Let's get the fuck out of here,' Sophie said. 'They're going to try and get me to sing.'

'Oh relax!' said Isaac.

'I'll go with you,' Wolf said to Sophie, and started to walk towards the door.

'Oh for fuck's sake,' Isaac said, following them.

Sophie was quiet, head down, ignoring the people who tried to talk to her as they walked up the steps and out past the bouncer.

They went up Sixth Avenue with the warm breeze in their faces and the cars zipping by at speed, Manhattan towering around them. He felt like he used to feel all the time in this city, that he could give himself over entirely to the next few hours. If he happened to survive them it was just because it turned out that way. Each particle of time represented only itself, which is to say it represented nothing, it wasn't laden with some past event, nor did it anticipate an occurrence which may or may not be in the future. It was pure present tense, pure time, absent of reflection; what a relief, like the light drizzle falling on his skin, it made him want to open his mouth to the sky. Isaac and Sophie had walked ahead and it sounded like they were fighting, or at least Isaac was, their voices coming back to Wolf in snatches in the breeze that was strong on his face. He came to a standstill, exhausted to the bone. When he closed his eyes the noise of the cars was a roaring ocean getting louder all around him, climbing above him, and for a moment he was on a beach in darkness, Miriam by his side. It is their honeymoon in Australia, and they have taken the beach route back to the hotel after the restaurant. They hold their shoes in their hands and the water is warm from the day of sun that is long gone. Even though they are right next to each other it is difficult to be heard above the crash of the ocean and for a few minutes they simply hold hands, standing in front of the magnificent dark mass of water. It is Byron Bay, the easternmost point of the continent. People come here on New Year's Eve to be the first to greet the future when it appears over the water's edge, burning and full of promise. He wants to believe there is nothing beyond the horizon, that they are at the edge of the known world, the point where the universe begins. They had deferred their honeymoon for five years. Just before leaving, Miriam found out she was pregnant with Ruth. So in fact the three of them are there together and it is a moment of elation and awe, undoubtedly the happiest of his life. The surf is pure white. It contains a recurring message just beyond his comprehension. You could stand there forever, waiting for the next wave, thinking you'll get it next time, whatever it is trying to tell you. But when he looks again Miriam is no longer standing by his side. The black ocean swells above him even larger. He closes his eyes tighter but she doesn't reappear. The ocean roars. It would be a simple thing to walk into it, allowing it to subsume him, which it seems to want to do, beckoning him towards it, pulling him with the breezes that are plainly under its control. He stares harder into the blackness. The exhaustion pushes him gently forward, the wind pulling at him, grasping at his hair and clothes, the strands of it fighting over him, the black water offering a simple answer to everything, to all his questions, with her silence. His name is being called. As far away as possible. *Wolfgang.* The voice punctuates the blackness and spreads out to an awakening. It's Isaac. When he opens his eyes, he and Sophie are standing waiting fifty yards ahead, and after a moment he makes an effort to walk in their direction. They have already started to walk on. He is staggering. The finality of Miriam's absence comes to him all at once as a difficulty breathing, a tonnage weight in the centre of his chest. The tears are flooding down his face, mixed with the warm rain. He would fall to his knees but his legs refuse to buckle. They move over the ground in dumb persistence, like a beast of burden that won't respond to commands. Isaac and Sophie are getting further ahead of him, they are almost out of sight.

8

'DID YOU HAVE a fight with Uncle Isaac or something?'

'You'll have to ask him.'

'I did. He told me you both drank too much. Which doesn't answer the question.'

'Look, I just fell awkwardly. Tripped, OK?'

He made an effort to smile, but he was irritated at the same time, and sore, the centre of his face dull with pain. He could barely breathe through his nose.

'My whole body aches,' he added, as if this was further proof.

'Is it broken?'

'What?'

'Your bloody nose for Christ's sake.'

'Just bruised I imagine.'

'You imagine? Didn't they tell you?'

'All they said was to ice it a few times a day and remove the packing after forty-eight hours.'

She seemed doubtful, and he would have produced the emergency room discharge instructions, but they were crumpled and blood-stained when he came across them earlier in the morning in his trouser pocket, and presumably he threw them away. Thankfully the waitress materialized. He looked down at his menu, but it was hard to make any sense of it. The waitress said she would give them another few minutes. The menu was annoying him, there were different sections to it. He folded it back up incorrectly and put it down. Ruth wasn't paying any attention to hers, but neither had she noticed the difficulty he was having, and was looking out at the room.

'What's in the bag?' he said to her, noticing what was on the chair beside her.

'You're joking, right?'

She was looking at him now.

'What is wrong with you?'

She let out a deep breath, the blank face of him looking back at her.

'They're Mum's ashes of course.'

'I don't recognize the bag, that's all.'

Another slight delay while she stared at him in disbelief.

'Well you gave it to me, Mike.'

Neither of them spoke for a while and there was just the background noise of the other customers gabbing away to each other. Ruth looked around the room.

'So this is where you did all your schmoozing then, is it?'

He also looked around the restaurant. It had been one of Miriam's old haunts, a place on the Upper West Side, on Amsterdam Avenue. It was all he could do to get Ruth to come into any restaurant with him, by dangling the ghost of her mother's youth in front of her. It was Yom Kippur, evidently a day of fast and prayer. Ruth wanted to observe it. She was emphatic about this when they had met earlier, outside the hotel. This is God's day, she told him, a day for repentance. Atonement. He had laughed but she wasn't being ironic. If anything she seemed righteous about it. Pity, he said. I wanted to bring you to one of Mum's places. *Where? Which one?* He saw that she was dressed quite formally, but there was also something else that was different about her appearance, that he couldn't quite put his finger on. Strangely, she had been sitting by herself in the back of a saloon car when he came out to meet her as arranged in front of the hotel. The manager intercepted him at reception and brought him out to her, then went off to get the driver. When he slid into the back seat beside her, Ruth didn't explain the car and Wolf didn't ask about it.

'Is it far this place?' she wanted to know.

'The Upper West Side.'

She relented. It was in the vicinity of where they were going in any case. Some synagogue apparently. But then it didn't help that he was vague in the directions he gave the driver, when he finally appeared, looking as if he was still finishing his breakfast as he walked towards them, chewing on something and adjusting his trousers. The manager stood at the entrance looking after them as they pulled off. Wolf thought all of this was odd – the car, the driver, the attentive manager – but Ruth seemed to take it in her stride. The driver acted as if he already knew him. His eyes studied Wolf in the mirror. Wolf ignored him and looked out the window in silence as they drove through Manhattan. The restaurant, when they finally located it, ended up being further uptown than he remembered. Ruth told the driver not to wait. They could walk to the synagogue from there.

'We can't stay long,' she said under her breath to him as the hostess led them to a corner table. 'They'll all be waiting.' He didn't ask who 'they' were.

When they took their seats Ruth let out a gasp.

'What?' he asked before realizing what the matter was. Her chair faced a wall of dogs. There must have been a thousand photographs of them. He remembered it now, the dogs. In actual fact it was the defining feature of the restaurant, the entire wall space was plastered with photos of every breed imaginable. They sat in silence. Ruth was wearing a light-coloured dress, almost cream, very uncharacteristic of her.

The waitress came back to their table and he ordered something without even checking the menu. Ruth handed hers back.

'I'm OK thanks.'

'Nothing?' said the waitress.

'I'm fasting,' Ruth said.

'It's Yom *Kipper*,' Wolf said, deliberately mispronouncing it. He laughed, but both Ruth and the waitress looked at him as if he was an idiot.

'Oh, bring her some coffee,' he said, handing his own menu to the waitress. 'You can have some of my pancakes,' he said, looking at Ruth. 'I won't tell Yahweh on you.'

Ruth shook her head.

'I'm really OK thanks,' she said to the waitress.

The waitress left them and his daughter looked around the restaurant. She was ignoring him entirely now. It gave him a chance to look around too, to check how familiar the place was. They were seated in the main room. It was only half full, possibly because of the religious holiday. The dogs were clearly making Ruth uncomfortable, literally every square inch of the walls was covered with them.

'I'd forgotten about that,' he said. 'The dogs.'

'As long as they're just photos.'

He laughed. Both of them were now staring at the wall nearest them, all the animals looking out at them. Ruth's facial expression was pure distaste and she gave a shudder. His daughter had always had a terror of dogs. She was never one of those children who wanted a puppy, or even a pony or a kitten for that matter. If anything, when she was young – and who knows, perhaps to this day – she had an attachment to the unwanted creatures of the world, the unthought of, slugs and the like, worms, particularly after heavy rainfall, when they would stupidly emerge onto the footpath as if they were going to find a haven there. Lacking in any hide or shell for protection, a pure innards of nerve endings, which didn't seem to end anywhere except on their skinless surface. As a child she would pick with great care her footsteps on the wet pavement, tiptoeing, distraught if she happened to squash one by accident. Sometimes she would pick them up and place them back in the grass, where no doubt they drowned slowly, cursing her from within the mesh of their subconscious. Dogs she hated though, it was their jaws of teeth, their propensity for aggression, even if it was simulated most of the time. They were all male to her, even the female ones.

'What did he say exactly? Isaac?'

'Just that you were drinking and . . .'

'What?'

'I got the impression that you were being an arse again.'

'Where?'

Ruth gave him a surprised look.

'What do you mean where? How should I know? I've been in Brooklyn the past three nights.'

He drank his coffee and looked around the restaurant. A woman across the way was filing her nails. She was by the window in the sun. Small cloud puffs emerged from her fingertips as she worked on them. He imagined the bone being sheared down, the fingers ground to stumps. *Three nights.* Did they not go to that other place yesterday? That building. And then there was last night. Surely she had been in the hotel room, he remembered it, she had complained about having to share a room with him. He said he would look into it in the morning, but he forgot. Three nights. He tried to take it in his stride. He was good at hiding that sense of shock which was becoming familiar to him now. It was like looking down to see part of the ground had given way, that rent in the fabric of things, a huge depth revealed without warning, but which had been there all along.

When he turned back to Ruth she was staring at him.

'You don't remember, do you?'

He started to say something but stopped. He didn't have

the energy to lie, or the patience. He was tempted to have an adult conversation with her, to lay it all out and spare her nothing, strip everything away, which was always his instinct anyway. He moved forward in his seat, wondering how to begin. But Ruth spoke first, she was angry.

'Christ. You're pathetic. Can't you just lay off the bottle, Mike? I mean, is it really that hard? What, should we be getting you some help?'

She looked away, shaking her head.

'Mike the alky. How embarrassing.'

Five, ten minutes must have passed without either of them speaking. Ruth continued to look around the interior of the restaurant, anything but at him. Wolf didn't care, he persisted in looking at her, no matter that it made her uncomfortable. One thing he could still clearly remember was holding her, just hours into her life. She was premature, barely bigger than his hand. Her skull, misshapen from the birth process, but which seemed to be correcting itself right in front of his eyes. The tiny weight of her. It could have been a few hours ago, yesterday, last week, there was no difference. He had a small burst of elation, but perhaps it was just exhaustion. He yearned to have a normal conversation with her, like any of the ones that seemed to be happening all around them. God knows what he would say, but he wouldn't have cared, it would feel good to let the words spill out of him. As ever, his voice was stuck, hesitant, awkward, and the moment passed, and the desire also then passed, leaving him only with his silence, which builds its own momentum. All he could do was look where Ruth was looking, at the bustling dining area, the dated interior of the restaurant, which had been one of Miriam's favourite brunch spots. Not for the first time that morning or even that hour, he felt with brief force the finality of his wife's absence from his life. It was almost entirely physical, his face was heating, he had to sit rigid, the arm and leg muscles gripping his bones, he was liable to slide into a shapeless pile on the floor otherwise. He opened his eyes. Ruth was staring over at the woman filing her nails, she was still working away on them, producing small clouds of dust, whittling her fingertips right down to the joints of the bone.

'This was one of the first places we went to,' he said, mainly to reset the tone a little. Mentioning Miriam was the only way he knew of doing this. 'Just after we met. For brunch.'

Ruth didn't react, but then she looked around the room as if expecting to see her parents sitting nearby as a young couple. Wolf noticed the bag on the chair beside them. He hadn't seen it before. He was about to ask Ruth about it but she was looking at him again.

'You had all this time with her.'

It was an accusation. But then her body language relaxed a touch and she just seemed immensely sad. She placed both elbows on the table.

'Before I was even born.'

He felt like he should say something comforting to her but he couldn't think of anything that wasn't patently false, so he just looked back at her. They had each had wildly differing roles in Miriam's life. It was self-evident really. Just because you are closely related to somebody – father or son or daughter or mother – doesn't mean that your lives aren't completely separate things.

'What would Mum order?' Ruth asked.

'Probably something with bacon on it.'

'No way!'

He picked up the menu.

'Things haven't changed that much I don't think, let me see if anything rings a bell.'

Ruth was silent again and he could tell she was looking at him, jealous again, possibly close to tears. He put down the menu.

'You look different,' he said to her, and as he said it he realized why. 'You're not wearing any make-up.'

'Or jewellery,' Ruth said, and he noticed that this was also true. She had even taken out her little nose stud. All in all she looked more grown-up, certainly less the child trying to be an adult. Even her clothes were relatively bright by her usual goth standards.

'It's Yom Kippur, Mike. You're not supposed to beautify yourself. Or have animal skin anywhere near you. You come as you are. Before God.'

He nodded. He didn't think he'd heard that before. Again there was no trace of irony in her voice.

'Since when are you so religious?'

'Since when are you nothing?' she said back to him.

'Since always,' he said. 'But nothing is not nothing.'

'Oh, very deep that is. Very deep indeed, Mike.'

He laughed.

'Mum wasn't religious,' he said.

'Only because of you.'

'Not true.'

'Yeah, well ...' Ruth said, but stopped, and she sat back in her chair with her arms folded. He recognized himself in her stumped response. Miriam would not have let him win so easily. More minutes of silence passed between them. The waitress came and apologized for the delay, topping up his coffee.

He remembered something and leaned over to Ruth, smiling at her. She looked alarmed.

'What?' she said again.

He continued to just smile at her.

'What?!'

He sat forward, placing his folded arms on the table.

'Isn't Yom Kippur the one where you have to ask me for forgiveness?'

Ruth looked back at him, horrified.

'Oh God.'

'Oh God,' she said again.

He laughed out loud at her plain discomfort. His daughter's face was bright red. He was obviously right. Yom Kippur was the one Jewish ritual that they had semi-followed each year in their house, at least in the early days when Ruth was little. Miriam used to go to the services at the West London synagogue in Marylebone, partly because they had a decent café there. This particular holiday was more meaningful to her than the other ones. She would even stand in front of him on the eve of Yom Kippur – Erev Yom Kippur – and fulfil in all seriousness the ritualistic requirement according to the Torah of asking those in her life for forgiveness, beginning with her husband. The first time he knew anything about it was a few months after they had initially met. He tried to cook her dinner in the sublet on Bleecker Street where he was living. It only dawned on him long afterwards that the reason Miriam couldn't eat the dinner he had made for her was not due to illness like she'd said, but because it was as far from kosher as you could imagine. He'd never known any Jewish people before.

'I need to ask you something,' Miriam said to him that night, after she had finished moving the food around on her plate, pretending both to eat and at the same time to be too ill to eat. (It looks lovely, she kept saying, it looks lovely.) She started explaining to him about Yom Kippur, the Book of Life, and the need according to the Torah to seek forgiveness from all the people in your life. She was rambling, and he smiled as he watched her, before she finally composed herself, closing her eyes for a long moment. She was wearing a long tight dress that came down over her feet. Her brown hair flowed and her inherent decency and kindness were no less obvious but seemed to enhance her physical appearance. Sometimes he thought she was the most beautiful woman he had ever seen. She opened her eyes again and looked directly at him.

'Will you forgive me?'

'Yes,' he said, and it struck him as the most serious thing he had ever said in his life up to that point.

But this practice, along with everything else, fizzled out during the early years of their marriage. Miriam tried to keep up some of the Jewish traditions. He never prevented or opposed any of it – on the contrary, he recalled being encouraging and even enjoyed the veneer of spirituality it added to his life. But it is simply too much effort when there is only one of you at it, Miriam saying the prayers the man was supposed to say, over the wine, for example, or praising the woman who prepared the meal, or singing by herself the various chants and songs that must have sounded so odd to her without the accompaniment of a room full of people chanting them together. How bereft and lonely this must have made her feel. You could tell that she felt foolish after-wards, and they mostly rushed through the Shabbat meals, and when the thing was finished, cleaning up, Miriam was always distant, frankly sad. He didn't think even now that there was much he could have done about it. The main bar-riers to tradition are not the ones you can easily see, the laws or edicts being pushed into your face, people like Avram standing on the fence, armed with their vehemence, their intolerance, their stridency. The main challenge rather is the slow apathy. The soft drift and erosion of time passing, and the process – painless, irreversible, silent – of becoming a different person entirely. It wasn't until Ruth got beyond the young child phase and became cogent and began to ask questions that Miriam started to get back into some of her traditions, Friday night Shabbat and the lighting of the can-dles, Yom Kippur especially, but also Rosh Hashanah, and even one or two of the more obscure holidays, of which there seemed to be hundreds, practically one a week. He wasn't around for any of this, but then last year Miriam called him out of the blue. He could hear his daughter protesting in the background, hammering on what he knew to be his old bedroom door.

'What are you saying to him, Mum?' he could hear her shouting. 'Don't ask him for forgiveness. Is that what you're doing? MUM!'

Miriam was sick but he didn't know it yet. This was a few weeks, perhaps a month or two, before Prague. Her voice was emotional on the other end of the phone. It wasn't like her and it made him concerned. If he didn't know better he would have thought she'd been drinking. She asked him for forgiveness and he said yes and then she was gone and he stood listening to the dead dial tone for a minute, before continuing on with things and then forgetting about it, except for a vague uneasiness that stayed with him for a while.

Ruth was still plainly uncomfortable.

'Don't worry,' he said to her. 'You don't have to ask me for forgiveness. It's OK. You can have it if you want it.'

'Thank God for that,' she said. But she also seemed genuinely relieved.

He allowed some time to pass. They settled back into their silence, Ruth looking around the room, while he continued to observe her. Yes, he could easily imagine her living here. New York would be a perfect fit for her. The Upper West Side in particular. She would have a good life once she got settled in, especially with a bit of money behind her. At least he could help with that much. And he knew that she would be ecstatic at the prospect of moving here. He couldn't wait to tell her. He tapped her on the elbow so that she turned around to face him.

'Hey,' he said. 'I was thinking. How would you like to live in New York?'

She looked back at him, more confused than anything.

'What are you talking about?'

She paused, before continuing, 'We've been through this, Mike, I told you what my plans are.'

He looked back at her, genuinely puzzled.

'For the umpteenth time, I don't want to live in New York. I'm serious. I'm going back to Israel. I've told you this twenty times. It's all I can do to get away from ... I don't know ... all this! OK?!'

He stared back at her.

'But you'll be able to be with your cousins. In Brooklyn. You can do the whole Jewish thing there, with them.'

Ruth was staring at him.

'The whole Jewish thing?'

He didn't say anything.

'They're not even properly Jewish,' she said. 'They don't obey kashrut. Josh even supports the BDS boycott for God's sake.'

'What about school?'

She exhaled loudly.

'Like I told you already, Mike, I'm going to do my A levels. I'm not stupid you know. But I'll be eighteen by then and I can do them over there. You can even get degrees and everything through the University of Tel Aviv. Organic agriculture, all sorts of stuff. There's tons of opportunities, much more than in the UK, all sorts of grants available for people like me. Returning Jews. Young people especially, who want to make aliyah.'

He was staring at her, at a complete loss.

She gave him a cold smile, as if she pitied him, her teeth showing.

'Don't worry, Mike. You'll have your freedom again. That's what you want, isn't it?'

9

THEY WALKED UP to 92nd Street even though it was twenty blocks. Ruth seemed happy for them to go at a relaxed pace. They didn't speak a single word the entire way, but there was no edge to their silence. It was the first morning they had so far encountered in which autumn could be discerned. The thick summer air of the previous days was now a little thinner and there was a taste, a certain unnameable smell, which spoke of the changed season. The breeze had more of an edge to it as it rattled the cage of the dying trees, causing their leaves to shed. People passing wore an extra layer of clothes. He noticed one or two faces turning to look at Ruth, and she was suddenly a striking sight, tall in her heels, pale, her hair long and full, that reddish tint to it. He was proud to be walking alongside her. He saw also how she would turn out, it was more than just a glimpse, here she was right beside him, the adult his daughter would become, and he knew that she would be fine, absolutely fine.

IO

THEY WERE ON time, even a few minutes early, but even so there they all were, standing waiting for them outside the synagogue. Avram, Allen and Judy and their four children – the smaller kids dressed in black waistcoats and white shirts – as well as Isaac and Max. Behind them various other groups congregated outside the front of the building. There was a small group of armed guards on the top steps surveying the crowd. Wolf and Ruth crossed the road and joined them.

Allen pointed at Wolf's face and said, 'How's this?'

Judy's face was full of concern.

'You have to be more careful,' she said.

Wolf wanted to ask her what she meant exactly. Ruth had already broken away from him and was standing to the side, more or less on her own.

'We're still headed to the kibbutz then, I take it,' Judy said to Wolf.

Both of them looked over at Ruth. The person closest to her was Isaac, who was also hanging back. He hadn't said hello to Wolf or even looked at him, but had retreated behind his partner, Max. Wolf was relieved to see Max, the only other non-Jewish person in the vicinity. He hadn't been inside a synagogue in twenty years and his memory of the experience was that it was a nice enough ceremony but he had felt self-conscious about his gentile status, as if it had been stamped on his forehead.

Ruth tapped Isaac on the arm.

'What's wrong with you?' she said to him, but he barely looked up from the ground. He was clearly in what Miriam used to refer to as his 'closed-off mode'. It was always one or the other with him, either the total extrovert who wouldn't shut up, or the way he was now – wronged, wounded, defensive. Wolf continued to look directly at him, but that only seemed to make him focus with more intent on the ground in front of him.

Avram clapped his hands and said, 'Come!' He then turned and walked in through the entrance past the security men. Judy removed some tickets from her bag and gave two to Wolf. He waited for Ruth and handed one of the tickets to her. They started to go inside, but Judy grabbed Wolf by his arm.

'Wait,' she said.

Everyone else went ahead of them.

'Allen told me,' Judy said.

Wolf looked at her, but had no idea what she was getting at.

'We need to talk,' she said. 'Not now, but we need to talk.'

Wolf nodded at her. She released him and they all went inside.

The ceremony was fine, even beautiful, but he couldn't stand to be in there for very long and left after forty-five minutes.

It was the same rabbi from the Tashlich and he sang for virtually the entire time, his voice filling the synagogue, amplified
by a small microphone that was clipped to his white shirt,
but also by the high walls and enormous vault-like space of
the building. A large group of musicians, several of them
children of all ages with triangles and bongo drums and
other semi-instruments, sat together off to the side of the
central table or altar where the rabbi and all his deputies
stood. Thankfully Judy had led them upstairs to sit on the
second level, over Avram's objections – he had wanted to
press all the way to the front row, from where escape would
have been much more difficult. They had a good view of the
synagogue's interior, which was beautiful, the walls ornately
decorated with gold lettering in Hebrew and various designs
in addition to the odd biblical scene. Overall the building
was warmer and less imposing, more eastern, than your average cathedral. But at the same time it was also more similar
than distinct. They sat on wooden pews. Ruth shook her
head when she saw him get up and leave.

Outside, the sun was up and strong, caught in the windscreens and reflected glass and metal of all the cars parked
along the street. The security guards in their expensive
suits congregated at the entrance talking in Hebrew. Wolf
could tell from their accents they were Israeli. They looked
lethal, their heads shaved, firearms appreciable beneath
their tight-fitting suit jackets. He stood to one side of the
entrance, his back against the wall, and closed his eyes. One
of the guards seemed to be telling a joke but the others kept

interrupting him. They were like little boys talking in a playground. A car drove by and the guards instinctively looked at it, interrupting their banter, two of them changing position slightly, standing off a few paces.

It was only then that Wolf spotted Max standing down the street a little, smoking, leaning back against the wall on the other side of the synagogue entrance. He went over to him. Max held out his packet of cigarettes and Wolf took one and Max lit it for him.

'So have they converted you yet?' Wolf said, but he had to repeat the question to him.

'Nah, man, they don't try to convert you,' Max said then, taking what Wolf had said at face value. 'Not unless you want to. You gotta be born into it.'

'This is true,' Wolf said, laughing, feeling giddy, perhaps from the hit of the cigarette.

Max looked at him.

'I'm sorry about your nose, man.'

Wolf looked back at him.

'You may not think it about Isaac,' Max continued, 'but what you say can really damage him, man . . . I have to pick up the pieces, you know? Sometimes it can take weeks.'

Wolf gave a little laugh. In actual fact that was exactly what he would have assumed about their relationship.

'Anyway,' Max continued, 'you stand up for yourself, I stand up for him . . . but at the same time I'm sorry, man.'

This was already more words than they had ever exchanged. Wolf looked down to see Max's hand extended towards him. It was large, like that of a construction worker, the fingers thick and hairy. They shook hands and Max seemed to relax immediately, leaning back against the wall.

'I also didn't mean to hurt you so bad,' he said. 'I was just trying to hold you back, you know. Separate the two of you.' He was a big guy Max, six foot anyway, powerfully built. 'But, man, I just connected.'

'What was it all about exactly?' Wolf said.

'Aw, it was just real personal, man.'

'I don't remember any of it,' said Wolf.

'Well I hit you pretty hard,' Max said, a trace of pride in his voice.

'No, that's not the reason,' Wolf said, laughing, still giddy from the cigarette.

Max just looked at him, confused. He took a drag from his cigarette, then closed his eyes.

Neither of them said anything for a while and they just stood with their backs against the wall, Max retreating back into his taciturn state, basking in the sun coming from that direction. Max was a total mystery to Wolf. There are some people who you could know for a hundred years and it wouldn't make any difference to the distance that still existed between you. There was never any prospect of getting beyond it, no getting closer. Miriam had always liked him though. He was the perfect match for her emotionally fragile brother, even if they were all a bit sketchy on the biographical details of his life, other than that he was from Central America and had come to the US illegally initially, twenty years ago, although that was never openly mentioned. Perhaps his status had changed in the meantime.

The security guards started laughing. They were like boys again, one of them in particular laughing hysterically. Wolf took a step out from the wall and looked back at Max. He still had his head resting against the wall, eyes closed in the sun.

'So what were we fighting about?' Wolf said to him now. Max opened his eyes. Possibly he had forgotten Wolf was still there.

'Aw, it just got real personal, man, y'know?' he said. 'All this shit about Miriam. Isaac saying you didn't treat her well, not as good as Noah. You know how he can get ... he wouldn't stop ...'

'Who's Noah?'

Max had an alarmed look on his face.

Wolf returned his gaze but didn't say anything.

'I don't know, man,' he said, then, 'I mean, talk to Ruth or Isaac ... He was just some friend to Miriam I think ... That's all I know. I only met him a couple of times.'

Wolf stood up straight. The cigarette was making everything spin. He hadn't smoked one in years. When he opened his eyes Max was looking at him, a concerned expression on his face.

'Look, man, I know Isaac can be an asshole ...' He didn't finish the sentence with any words, but rather continued looking at him intently. He took another drag from his cigarette. A stretch limousine drove by and both of them followed it with their eyes as if it was something that had come from another world. The Israeli security guards also looked at it. Max put his cigarette on the ground and pressed his foot on it. Then he put his hands in his pockets and said, 'Cold', even though it was not particularly. Another few moments passed and Max announced that he was going to head back inside.

I I

WOLF WALKED IN the direction of Amsterdam Avenue. Once he got to the corner he turned and went uptown and crossed the avenue, heading eastwards towards Broadway. He couldn't remember the exact address of the apartment Miriam lived in when he had first met her but he was pretty sure he would recognize it if he came across it; 94th Street seemed about right and he went along it. There weren't many people about, just the odd person pushing a stroller or sitting out on the steps of their brownstone, a jogger with a dog, a man wearing a skullcap headed in no great hurry no doubt to the place he himself had just left. He took his time, paying attention to the buildings. There was an unevenness to the brownstones, some of them redolent of pure wealth and exclusivity while others were run-down, presumably rent-controlled, split into flats, dozens undoubtedly living there. This unevenness gave the street the appearance of being cramped, as if the original builders had decided at the last minute to squeeze an extra few houses into the terrace. You got glimpses in through the windows as you went, mostly of empty rooms, some soul sitting by the window or on his couch, alone, nothing for company, maybe a cat, peeking over the sill or laid out on the ledge in the early-afternoon sun, which was strong, albeit heatless. Cars were tightly parked, leaving room only for the occasional hydrant. Their windscreens faced towards him, their planes of glass lighting up as he went by.

And then he recognized it, Miriam's old condo building. He felt a small burst of elation, he couldn't believe that he'd found it. From the outside it looked like it was still comprised of apartments. A small knee-high fence demarcated the outer border of the property. He turned into the short path towards the door. Names were handwritten in biro beside each of the buzzers, and even this was familiar to him. He stood for a moment. The ridiculous thought came to him that it was only a matter of hitting the right buzzer and Miriam would come down the steps and greet him. He rang the doorbell of the top apartment. The intercom didn't respond, so after a minute he rang it again. He closed his eyes and listened for the internal sounds of the house. A woman's voice, a crying baby from an open window in the building next door. Music from the radio of a car which turned the corner and drove behind him. Other sounds further off. Nothing from the house itself. He closed his eyes tighter. If he concentrated enough he could will his brain to hear once again the door of Miriam's apartment close – she always slammed it clumsily after her, half the time forgetting to take her keys with her – then seconds later her footfall on the creaking stairs which ended just on the other side of the front door.

And then he did hear a door slam and steps on the stairs. He felt the old excitement, the anticipation, and he thought, it's just memory leaking out of me, putting me back there. That's the way it felt sometimes, not that his memory was being attacked or had eroded, but rather that it was being lost steadily through some hole in the mind, leaking out, but for an instant surrounding him in a thick gauze of recollection, overwhelming in its clarity and vividness, before dissipating altogether. The steps were getting louder and now the inside of the door was being fiddled with to get it open, something else Miriam would always struggle with. The latch gave and the door was being pulled back and he closed his eyes again very briefly and tightly one more time, every sensation in his body primed to see Miriam appear before him.

'Yes?'

'Miriam.'

He opened his eyes. A man was standing there. Youngish, with a tightly cropped beard, a white shirt.

'My wife Miriam,' Wolf said. 'She used to live here. Twenty years ago.'

The man's hand was keeping the door open, he could easily close it.

'Let me start again,' Wolf said, and he made an effort to regain his composure, holding up his hand, laughing a little, an attempt at charm even.

'First of all, I'm very sorry to bother you,' he said. 'It's just that my wife used to live here you see. Twenty years ago. I don't live in New York any more, but I was in town, as you can see, and I was wondering if there was any possibility of having another look at the apartment, for memory's sake...'

The man continued to say nothing and just stared back at him.

'It's a strange request I know,' Wolf said. 'I understand if you're too busy, or if now is not a good time.'

The man continued to look at him.

'It's just that she died recently . . .'

'Sure,' the man said then, quickly, his decision made. 'I get it. It's the sort of thing I would ask myself actually . . . Besides, I'm getting no work done.'

He stood back and opened the door wider to let Wolf in, putting his back up against it.

'I really appreciate this,' Wolf said, and he went inside.

The hallway was dark and unfamiliar, even though it didn't look as if it had been renovated recently or was new. It was only when he stepped onto the stairs that the knowledge that this was Miriam's old place shifted from pure intellectual memory to something that was more immediate, beyond any doubt.

'I keep meaning to get the intercom fixed. Otherwise I could have buzzed you in.'

'Or not.'

'Yeah I guess. It's harder to say no when you're F2F, right?'

Now it was Wolf's turn to laugh at the man's inane acronym, a new one on him. They continued up the stairs.

'They haven't renovated the place I see. You don't own it?'

'The apartment, yeah. But the building is a mess. Bit of an issue for us, an ongoing thing, a battle or whatever.'

They arrived on the top floor.

'Well, here we are,' said the man and he took out his keys and opened his door. Number 43. Wolf remembered the hallway outside now, mostly the mustiness of the old carpet, which hadn't been changed in twenty years. The man pushed open the door and then held it for Wolf and he walked in.

The room was full of light and – he knew it straight away – totally unrecognizable. When Miriam lived here the living room had been divided into two bedrooms to make four in total. The effect had been to block out all the natural light and the apartment was always in darkness, dependent entirely on the low-wattage lights, which were permanently on. Miriam's flatmate Ruth had been a fixture on the couch, typing away on her Mac, it seemed that she never left the place.

'Well, you're welcome to have a look around,' said the man, and he walked over to his desk on the right-hand side of the room. It was a large drawing desk, tilted at an angle, facing towards the far window, a high stool behind it.

Wolf walked towards the window. The apartment now comprised a reasonably large open-plan room. It was clear that money had been sunk into the place. A small kitchen stood to the right side, in the same position as it had been previously, but now it was part of the room, the wall having also been knocked down. The remaining walls had been painted white and the old carpet was gone, replaced by wooden floors which were darkly varnished. It was a successful renovation job, leaving nothing of the past, as if the past was an infectious disease that had been stamped out, fumigated from the building's substance and structure. A corridor led off to the left, presumably towards the bedroom and bathroom, but he didn't need to go there. Miriam's old bedroom was right here where he was standing, but he could have been standing anywhere. He said it to himself a few times. *Right here. Right here.* As if the words were a spell. But if they were, they had lost their power, there was no particular resonance to them, no memories assailed him.

'It won't be the way you remember it, that's for sure,' the man said. He seemed proud. He was sitting up on his stool, his arms folded.

'You did it yourself?'

'Yep. Everything.'

Wolf looked down at the floor. Not a single thought entered his mind.

'Every now and again I compare it to photos of the way it was,' the man said. 'I wanted to make it like this when we bought it.' He pointed downwards at the paper on his sloped desk. Wolf took a few steps towards him and saw that he was pointing at a large blank sheet of paper, not even a pencil mark made on it.

'Exactly like this,' he said, and again there was that pride.

Wolf continued to stare down at the blank paper. It caught the sun and hurt his eyes.

'The windows are the cardinal feature,' the man said, and Wolf raised his head to look at what he was now indicating. 'It amazes me that people don't understand that about these old buildings. You can see the park.'

Wolf took a couple of steps towards the window and stood for a moment. Then he turned around.

'I really thank you for your time. No small thing in this day and age.'

The man shrugged and stood up and they went towards the door. Something occurred to Wolf and he turned to the man.

'Those photos you mentioned?' he asked him. 'Do you still have them by any chance?'

The man didn't say anything but moved over to a shelving unit just inside the door which Wolf hadn't noticed before. He pulled a large plastic box halfway off the shelf, supporting it with his knee. After rooting about in it for a minute he took out a handful of loose Polaroids.

'Here,' he said, handing Wolf one of them. 'I must be one of the only people on the planet still using Polaroids.'

Wolf looked down at the photograph. The image had been taken from the vantage point of the door. The dividers were there and the far window was just a sliver of light. But you could make out the way the room had once been. The basic structure of it.

'That's it,' Wolf said. 'That's the way I remember it.'

'It was like a lot of work,' the man said, 'to get from there to here.'

Wolf handed him back the photo, but the man waved him away with his hand.

'Take it. I got duplicates.'

Wolf said thank you and put the photograph in his inside pocket.

The man walked down the stairs with him. He said he was going to go to the bodega on the corner anyway. When they opened the front door of the main house a woman was approaching it pushing a stroller. The man called out to her and it was obvious it was his wife. She looked at Wolf. She was a blonde, attractive woman. When she saw him there was a look of recognition on her face, her smile fading.

'Hello again,' she said. She looked at her husband, who appeared confused.

'You're back,' she said, and now it was Wolf's turn to be at a loss.

'What do you mean?' the man asked her, then turned to look at Wolf also.

'He came here with his daughter the other day,' she said, 'to have a look around. I came home and they were standing here looking up. His wife lived in our apartment once. Apparently.'

The man looked at Wolf, his face forming a question. Wolf returned his gaze as openly as he could, but he didn't know what to say. Just then his phone started to ring in his pocket.

'I have to go,' he said, 'thank you again,' and he took out the ringing phone and held it up to them as evidence. He took a few steps down the small path and answered it. The man and his wife just stood there, looking after him.

'WHERE ARE YOU?'

He didn't reply.

'We're all here,' Ruth said. 'Waiting. Even the rabbi.'

'Where?'

'What?!' said Ruth, incredulous. 'Please tell me you have Mum's ashes. Christ.'

Wolf looked down. He was carrying a bag.

'Yes, of course. I meant whereabouts. Specifically.'

Ruth sighed loudly into the phone.

'Just across from the 96th Street exit. You can't miss us. Everyone's here. Apart from you that is.'

I 2

THEY WERE STANDING around waiting for him at the water's edge. All of Allen and Judy's children, family friends and others, the majority really, who didn't even look familiar to him. Everyone looked in his direction as he walked over from where the taxi dropped him off, down the steps and across the wide verge of grass to the water's edge, although nobody apart from Ruth came towards him.

'Give me the bag,' she said when they were ten, fifteen feet apart. He hadn't realized he was holding it so tightly until she wrenched the bag from him.

'Thank fuck you didn't lose them.'

'At last, finally he arrive!' Avram shouted out. He was standing with two people who looked vaguely familiar to Wolf – a grey-haired man and a woman wearing a blue and white skullcap. There was another younger man with them, he was also wearing one. Wolf could tell right away he was their son. He seemed to be staring at Wolf with great interest.

The rabbi came over and shook Wolf's hand and introduced herself. She was a very tall woman with jet black hair. She was wearing a white robe and a small bright blue yarmulke, her skin was very pale. Miriam had booked her online on the basis of her website, which was as non-denominational as you could get. She specialized in the standard rituals but with a twist to them in terms of their context: gay weddings, inter-religious ceremonies, cremations, even animal burials – anything needing the imprimatur of Godness not otherwise available. She and Miriam spoke by Skype on a couple of occasions.

The rabbi sympathized with him about Miriam and said that even though she never met her in person she felt that she knew her really well. Then she got down to business.

'So if you stand over here,' she said, walking towards a small table that she had set up by the water's edge, covered by a white tablecloth. Wolf and Ruth followed her.

'And Ruth will be beside you,' she said, taking Ruth by the hands and pulling her over.

She turned and addressed the gathering in general, spread out in small groups.

'Now if you could all gather around,' she said, before repeating it louder a few times to get everybody's attention.

Eventually they did all gather around and the hum of conversation stopped. He could feel the press of the small crowd behind him. He looked beyond the rabbi to the flowing, smooth river which was a pretty light-filled grey, geometric shapes of sunlight appearing and reappearing across its surface.

'We have come here today,' the rabbi said, 'to scatter the ashes that are all that now remain of the body of Miriam. In a beautiful and ancient rite, we have given her body to the flames and now we give it to the water. Fire is the visible form of energy, the true essence of all that appears in this world where we express ourselves through bodies and minds, until at last all that is left is this handful of ash.'

She lit a candle using a long taper, struggling to get the little flame going in the light river breeze. Wolf closed his eyes and concentrated on the breeze on his face. He only opened them when the rabbi started once more to speak.

'These ashes are not Miriam. They are merely what remains of the body she wore at the close of her sojourn here on this earth. Miriam had many bodies. First she had the body of an infant, then of a girl, then of a grown woman, and finally, this body that we have returned to the fire, to the air, to the waters of the earth and to the earth itself.'

She broke into song then, singing something in Hebrew that was beautiful. She had a good strong voice. Wolf closed his eyes and listened. There were other sounds but they all blended together – the odd voice going by behind them on the path talking into a phone, a boat's horn on the river, the drone of cars above their heads on the Henry Hudson. The rabbi finished her song and then continued speaking:

'In the warm sunshine of this late-summer day, we scatter Miriam's ashes on her beloved Hudson on the anniversary date of her birth. No longer bound by this world, but a part of it. No longer tied to one place, one time, but free. Every time you feel the warm sunshine on your face, every time you hear the rain softly falling outside your window, no matter where you are, no matter how far you travel in this big, wide-open world, remember.'

The rabbi indicated for both Ruth and Wolf to come to the water's edge and bade them take the urn in both their hands and scatter the ashes into the water.

'If you come closer,' she said to everyone, 'we will now perform the scattering of the ashes.' He felt the pressure of the crowd gathered behind them and he was grateful for their presence.

The rabbi said aloud, 'At the rising of the sun and at its going down . . .'

'We will remember her,' everyone answered.

'At the blowing of the wind and in the chill of winter . . .' the rabbi said.

'We will remember her.'

'At the opening of the buds and in the rebirth of spring . . .'

'We will remember her.'

And so they continued, as Ruth and he scattered the ashes of her mother, his wife. The rabbi led the crowd, and among them he could make out the voices of Avram and Isaac and even Max.

'At the blueness of the skies and in the warmth of summer . . .'

'We will remember her.'

'At the rustling of the leaves and in the beauty of autumn . . .'

'We will remember her.'

'At the beginning of the year and when it ends . . .'

'We will remember her.'

'When we are weary and in need of strength . . .'

'We will remember her.'

'When we are lost and sick at heart . . .'

'We will remember her.'

'When we have joy we crave to share . . .'

'We will remember her.'

'When we have decisions that are difficult to make . . .'

'We will remember her.'

'When we have achievements that are based on hers . . .'

'We will remember her.'

'As long as we live, she too will live . . .'

'We will remember her.'

13

THEY HEADED BACK along the riverside walkway. The group had mostly dispersed and gone their separate ways, and those who remained strolled in a file of twos and threes. They weren't going anywhere in particular, just in the direction of downtown along the redeveloped Hudson Riverside Park, with its inviting lush grassy areas, people sitting out on blankets, runners, rollerbladers, cyclists flying by them on the narrow pathway, the river right there, practically lapping at their ankles in places. Wolf made sure he was walking with Ruth, and he managed to put some distance between them and the others. Ruth was due to stay the night in Brooklyn.

'Who was that man you said goodbye to at the end?' he asked her. 'You were both crying. He seemed really upset.'

His daughter didn't respond.

'He was wearing a skullcap,' Wolf added.

'Yarmulke, Mike, is the technical term for it. Or kippah, if you'd prefer.'

'He was standing with that elderly couple. The woman was wearing one as well, a blue and white one. I've seen her before somewhere. He's their son, right?'

'Yes.'

'What's his name?'

Ruth paused before answering.

'Noah.'

'What?'

'Noah.'

'He was a friend of Mum's?'

She mumbled something.

'What?'

'More or less,' she said, her voice raised. This was clearly the last thing she wanted to talk about. She looked out over the water and they didn't speak for some time. They walked on. The sky was pale and cloudless. Ruth's face remained turned outwards to the river.

'He seemed really upset.'

'Well, it was that sort of occasion, wasn't it?'

Wolf stopped walking and tugged on her arm to make her turn around.

'Look, I don't mind,' he said. 'I'd like to know. Was he someone important to your mother?'

Ruth made an audible breath. He looked at her chest rise and gently fall. She was looking anywhere but at him.

'It's not what you think,' she said. 'He was like totally in love with Mum for years. It's actually very romantic. They knew each other since they were like two years old.'

'What happened?'

'Jesus Christ, Mike, you know all this!'

'Well maybe I've forgotten.'

Another deep breath.

'When Mum got sick she didn't want to see him any more. She called you instead for some reason. Much to everyone's surprise. She wanted you back in the picture. For my sake apparently. So in other words it was all my fault that they broke up. Another thing to make me feel good about myself.'

She walked on and he followed her. The path changed to a wooden surface, which extended right over the water for a section. It seemed to be undulating under him, as if they were moving across the deck of a large boat. For a second he became unbalanced. It stopped him dead and he needed to concentrate in order to continue. He felt slightly nause-ated. He undid his shirt some more, needing to take in air. Ruth was a little distance ahead of him but he caught up with her. She hadn't noticed anything. Her attention was fixed on the quiet expanse of the Hudson reaching across to New Jersey and opening out towards the unseen Atlantic. The zip of cars to their left was as constant, as loud as ever. They walked some distance before speaking again. Ahead of them the silent enormous skyscape emerged out of downtown Manhattan, where they seemed to be headed. It was dom-inated by the unfinished Freedom Tower with its thorned crown of cranes and scaffold.

'We might stay on in New York a bit,' he said. 'If that's OK.'

The words barely made it out of him. Ruth didn't notice that either, their thinness, the physical effort he had to make in order to speak. She stopped, turning to look at him, full of suspicion.

'Why?'

'Why not? We're having a good time, right? I'd like you to spend more time with Mum's family. Get to know them.'

'I already know them,' she said and then made a motion with her hand. 'Tick.'

'Well, you can get to know them a bit better.'

'Why?'

'Why not?'

'How long? What about all my stuff? I'll have to go back and get it.'

'You can manage for now. I'll buy you whatever you need.'

'I'm not staying at that hotel. I can stay with Ingrit in Brooklyn.'

'You can stay in Brooklyn, but it will have to be with ... the family.' The names didn't come to him and Ruth noticed this.

'Judy and Allen,' she said.

She was staring at the side of his face. He looked beyond her, out to the water. The sun was a red sphere above the palisades and the water was calm, the same colour as everything else. It was beginning to give everything, even the buildings, a bluish tinge. They walked on.

'Is this because of Israel?'

What she said confused him a little.

'I'm definitely going, you know. Once I'm eighteen. You can't stop me, legally.'

He looked her in the eye.

'It has nothing to do with Israel.'

Ruth was staring at the side of his face. She had a hundred questions occurring all at once and they rendered her completely mute.

'Why are you being all weird?' she said then. 'Are you in some kind of trouble, Mike?'

He laughed. That tone of hers.

'You never met your grandmother, did you? My mother.'

'You keep asking me that. For the twentieth time no, I mean, sorry, but no I never met your mother.'

'You would have liked her I think, maybe feared her a little, she could be fierce. Before her deterioration that is, when she totally lost her personality, who she was. There was no point to anything then. She became a total shell.'

'Again, Mike, you keep telling me all this,' Ruth said. 'I mean, I'm sorry and all, but – what's going on?'

'Nothing.' he said. 'I don't know, I'm just ...'

She looked at him and for a second it seemed that she understood everything. But then she broke out into a smile.

'What is it, Mike, are you trying to have a significant moment? Is that what this is?'

He laughed, genuinely. But he was bitterly sorry that just this once he couldn't cut through the thick shell of his daughter's irony, to speak to her plainly for once. He started to say something in that direction but stopped. He knew that if he continued to talk he would ramble. In any case, none of what he was saying was meant to be understood, at least not for now. Your best hope is for snatches of it to be remembered. So on they walked, and he hoped the silence would be articulate enough, along with the beauty of the evening, and also of course the added context of what they had both done not long ago further up the river bank. They continued on, both of them looking out over the smooth, still Hudson.

After a while Ruth wanted to stop and wait for the others. They'd made it all the way down beyond Midtown to the thirties. Everyone was a good distance back. It was Judy holding things up. She was a very slow walker, linking arms with one of her children. Even from here you could tell that Avram was impatient, stopping to turn and complain.

Wolf looked at Ruth's face as she looked back at them, her new family. She'd be fine with them, they'd take good care of her. In her expression and in the way she held herself she very much resembled her mother now. The reddish tinge to her hair was enhanced by the evening light. He continued staring at her, not caring if she noticed. Yes, she'd be just fine without him. He saw it perfectly clearly. She was even smiling with some affection at the group as they came towards them, but were still some distance away. They were chattering away among themselves now, no doubt discussing a shortlist of recurring complaints, their allergies, the humidity, any number of health anxieties or phobias, Judy waving her hands as she spoke, Allen patient, both of them lagging behind her grandfather Avram, her saba, who was no doubt grumbling, he had no patience for their prattle, their hypochondrism, which exasperated him thoroughly. Ruth wasn't going to admit it to Wolf, but all of a sudden she was quite excited about the prospect of hanging around Brooklyn for a while. She'd see more of Ingrit for starters, get more involved with the activities of the Chabad House, attend the Friday-night services which were her favourite, the wine, the singing, the sense of community, that's what *he* didn't get, what he could never understand. So she allowed herself to get momentarily giddy with the anticipation. She would be a New Yorker, just like Mum. But when she turned towards him her facial expression changed and she was looking at him in horror. It took him a second to realize why. The dark drops on the grey surface at his feet made him realize tears were running down his face. He didn't care. Let them fall. He felt depleted. There was nothing left and she might as well see this, it was after all what he was at the end of the day, a crying man who regretted almost everything.

Goodbye, Ruth, he said, but the words didn't make it. I love you, he said, but this too seemed to vanish as soon as he said it, carried off by the brisk breeze, the sounds of the world around them. He leaned in and gave his beautiful daughter a hug, and then he turned and hurried away.

14

HE MET A psychiatrist once, at a dinner party, the brother of a woman he was seeing at the time. They were sitting across from each other and the conversation was stilted. The dinner party was at the woman's flat; she was a failed writer who lived alone, she didn't care any more and her apartment reeked of the three or four small dogs she kept. There was to be nothing lasting between them and it had seemed to Wolf that everyone sitting around the table knew this, most of all the woman herself, who could not have been less bothered and sat up the other end, well away from him. It was probably one of the things which attracted him to her, that she saw through everything, and that to her, all was cause for amusement. Out of the blue the psychiatrist started to tell him about a patient he had seen that afternoon. He said the patient was a teenager who had recently been diagnosed with schizophrenia. You could talk normally with him without thinking anything was wrong, he said, until the young man's delusion – which was very particular, very specific – became apparent, and then he required continual reassurance. What was the nature of the delusion? Wolf asked. The psychiatrist laughed. That the world was going to throw him a party. He looked at Wolf and shook his head. That the entire world was going to throw him a party. Can you imagine? Nobody else at the dinner table was listening to them. The woman he was seeing was talking to the man beside her, another failed writer apparently – they got together in the weeks afterwards, he later heard. The idea absolutely fucking terrified him, the psychiatrist continued. That was the only reason the kid brought it up. And he keeps bringing it up the more time you spend with him, until you finally appreciate it, how sick he is, how deluded, it maybe wasn't so clear at first. He keeps wanting you to reassure him. That this is not going to happen. But there he is, absolutely terrified by the notion that the entire world, everyone in it, is going to get together somehow and, bang, he turns the corner or whatever and, SURPRISE, a party all for him, thrown by the entire world! The psychiatrist was distracted by someone across the table. Wolf sat thinking about the guy's patient. He could picture him actually, he could even picture the scene, the party the kid dreaded so much, the millions and millions of people waiting for him to show up, to come around the corner so they could greet him, in Hyde Park or wherever it was. Wolf felt for this kid, he felt that he might even understand where he was coming from. Maybe the kid wasn't all that deluded. That his vision was in the least description of it a form of reckoning, grotesquely exaggerated but otherwise on point; that the eyes of the world were on him, their judgement, their approbation, he merely seemed in terror of what the rest of us view as contingent, what we expect in the end to intervene on our behalf, before the veil falls, before you hit the water that is coming hard at you as the bridge far above recedes, that before the ultimate eventuality you will be pulled back somehow, the surprise being that in the end we all expect to be delivered and it turns out that all along we were believers. He may have been mulling all this over as the psychiatrist turned back to him to continue with the anecdote. He isn't happy, this kid, until you tell him, and I mean *really* swear it to him, as vehemently as you can, repeatedly, over and over, that the world is actually indifferent. That there will be no party. Only then is the lad relieved. But the relief only lasts a short interval and you can practically see the anxiety welling up in him again, his face trembling with it, and you have to emphasize it once more, I mean *really* emphasize it, to the point of being a bit brutal towards him, telling him over and over how little anyone cares about him and his situation, so that you're basically shouting at him, roaring at the top of your voice, and he's sitting there lapping it all up, the relief seeping into the cracks of his skin, his acne, which is really bad by the way, bearing the brunt of your voice, as you rail at him that no one cares, no one gives a shit, it's just you, mate, you're on your own, there ain't nobody else, nobody gives a damn, and why should they anyway, look at you, what you are, what you've become, the state of you. And the more you go on like that the more relieved he gets. So relieved that you'd never guess what?

What?

I swear to God the poor kid breaks out into the biggest smile you've ever seen. It is absolutely freaky, the psychiatrist said, but at the same time quite simply the *purest* vision of contentment you will ever see.

15

HE WAS GETTING his things together when there was a knock on the door. A man in a suit who seemed to know him. The name badge said Exec. Manager and he was wondering if he could have a word. It wouldn't take long. No, no, downstairs if possible. If he didn't mind that is. It will only take a minute and really it would be better down in the office. Nothing is the matter, really. Everything is fine. Your daughter is fine, absolutely fine, it isn't about her, it's another matter entirely. The man was looking beyond Wolf, he noticed his things on the bed. Is sir checking out? More or less, Wolf replied. The man stepped back and Wolf followed him, the door slamming shut behind him.

All there was to do then was to wait. He didn't know for how long. It could have been an hour or it could have been much longer than that. Really there is little difference between the two, especially in the absence of some action, going from one place to another, interacting with anyone. When it's just you sitting there with nothing to indicate the passing time, each moment slides indistinguishably into the next, just the passing stream of your thoughts wandering on their own path. Especially if you're sitting in a room such as this one with no natural light, it appeared to be an office of some sort, but he had no idea who it belonged to as it was bare with no personal indicators, photographs for example, and Wolf had the feeling that it didn't belong to anyone. A digital clock blinked at him from the desk but was stuck on the same numbers and they were so bright it was hard to credit what they were telling him. On the back wall was one of those things. The word was stuck. One of those things. It displayed the months and the year.

It came as a surprise then when Isaac appeared at the door. He pretended to have been expecting him all along. Maybe it had been him who had called him and told him to come meet him here. Just as surprising was Isaac's manner. Austere, grim like a pall-bearer. He didn't say much, but neither did he seem put out or annoyed. He was simply there to get Wolf. It was at Ruth's behest apparently. And Judy's. They wanted to talk with him. They were in Judy's house in Brooklyn. Judy, Wolf repeated slowly. Isaac looked at him. There was no sign of the Exec. Manager. Wolf sat back down on his chair and leaned against the wall behind him. He was exhausted. Calendar! He practically shouted the word out with relief. Isaac was looking at him again. Don't sit, we have to go, he said. He was holding the door open. Wolf followed him down the corridor. When the door of the lift opened they got in, emerging at reception. Isaac led him out to a car and put him into the back seat.

16

AT THE MEMORY clinic he attends the consultant likes to talk about hard memory and soft memory. He's a music fan, an art fan, this doctor, and he likes to give little seminars, thinking that Wolf cares about the explanations for things when really it's not the way his mind works at all. If the doctor had ever met Miriam he would have said that the doctor had conflated them, but he had never met her and Wolf finds the whole thing patronizing. He wants the guy to just fix him or lie to him and he is only ever there because there is no alternative other than to not go of course. The hard parts, the consultant continues, are verifiable, assessable by various types of audit and questionnaire, and here he must be referring to the tests they perform on Wolf to assess his cognitive state, ridiculously simple questions which irk him every time they subject him to them, just after they take his blood pressure and pulse, writing the results on a sheet of paper which they place on the desk for the consultant. Who is the prime minister? What day of the week is it? What year? Where are you right now, this very moment? I am going to tell you three words and I want you to remember them. Who am I? Have we met before? Who are you? Who is that person standing over there? Can you count backwards in sevens beginning at one hundred? What were those three words I told you a minute ago?

Soft memory is what we are made of, what forms us, how we view the past, which is really astonishing when you think about it, I mean really think about it, just a constellation of neuronal activity, a cluster of cell signalling, which generates pictures, fictional ones, unreliable obviously – how could they not be? – and associative emotions induced by those events which leave a residue, not all of them do, in truth probably only a small fraction of them, the fact is that the vast majority of our experiences pass like a flow of water that we never step into twice. He is grinning at Wolf now. Please. Not the fucking river analogy. I am tired and I just want to go home. Miriam will get suspicious if I'm not back. Wolf feels a sudden lurch of hatred for the doctor, but just as quickly this abates and he is exhausted. The consultant continues. For memory to become consolidated – he is now leaning forward with his elbows on the table – for memory to linger long enough in order to be hardwired into your brain, the amygdala to be precise, it's a process which requires a few hours. Or so the latest research tells us. If a normal person is distracted before that process completes itself the memory won't form. He pauses, looks at Wolf. A dramatic, irritating pause. This dude would have made a great ham actor. Finally the consultant puts him out of his suspense.

It is the cardinal feature of your condition, the doctor says.

Or at least it will be in time, once you have entered the

more advanced stage, the impaired ability to form *consolidated* memories.

The doctor sits back in his chair, perhaps aware that he has overdone it, sensing Wolf's irritation.

Still, part of him is hoping the guy will continue. It is hard to turn off that part of your brain which is always on the lookout for encouragement. The doctor smiles. He leaves it at that, and so it goes until the next time.

17

HE CAN RECALL that they drove in silence and darkness. He is sure that it was the West Side Highway. The Henry Hudson Parkway. He remembered wanting to say it out loud, proud that the words had come to him. Isaac is driving, hunched over the wheel, his hands rigid on it, concentrating hard, like someone not used to driving. He can recall the hum of the car engine and the transient noise of other vehicles overtaking them with ease. Avram is in the back seat alongside him, looking out his window, his hand resting in the space between them. He can recall that they are all spent somehow, as if this is the aftermath of some drama that he can't remember. And somehow he knows that they are all thinking of Miriam. You can virtually feel her presence. She is in their breathing, the air that surrounds them, and which is seeping into their bodies through their lungs. It is a moment of perfect calm, what other people perhaps mean by prayer or Godfulness, that has descended over them. Even Isaac is perfectly silent, his hands rocking gently from side to side on the steering wheel like the captain of a ship out on a dark and even sea. Avram's breathing has a slight whistling to it, as if he is asleep. But his eyes are wide open, looking out his window, and covered by a film of liquid. It is only when Wolf sees the moisture on his cheeks that he realizes he is weeping to himself. There is no sign of Ruth, but he resists the urge to ask about her. For as long as he can he allows himself to imagine that he is dead, looking down on this scene externally from the vantage point of his presence or absence, it doesn't matter which. He floats in and out of it in a silent buoyancy. He turns and looks out his own window over the Hudson, which is as black as the Styx, and at the night lights on the opposite New Jersey shore and, this side, at those of Manhattan, each of its buildings a shattering of light, perfectly contained, and spread out on the black water that he looks out on, illuminating the surface. Somehow he knows how it will go now. He wishes only that he retains for as long as possible the central part of what he has left, the core paradise of his memory, her shape, the outline of her kindness.

18

HE IS SITTING at a kitchen table when Ruth appears in the room. There is a mug of coffee in front of him. The house is not empty, every now and then there are noises from far off. Child's laughter. A voice telling them to shush. A door slams. Ruth doesn't take her eyes off him even for a second. She approaches him the way you stalk someone far bigger than you but you are confident nonetheless. She pulls out the chair across from him and sits down. She is still staring at him, no emotion, just fierce, a wall of questions challenging him, like many small faces embedded into a rock that rears above him.

'Were you going to top yourself?'

He doesn't say anything, but he knows that that isn't going to cut it.

'You heard me. Were you planning to top yourself?'

She stops, not taking her eyes off him.

'Your ex told us. Debra? She was there the other day, apparently. At Mum's ceremony. She called Judy afterwards.'

His body language expresses confusion, blankness.

'It all made sense then. Your weirdness. The way you were acting.'

Again, she got nothing back from him.

'Just in case you've forgotten,' she said, 'it was Saba and Uncle Isaac who brought you to the hospital. Some clinic somewhere. And now you're here. Do you remember *any* of this, Mike?'

Hospital. He can only think of the one they had brought Miriam to. That is his wife's name. Miriam. She has reddish hair, although he doesn't know where she is. Is she still sick? He remembers that she was wearing an oxygen mask and barely able to lift her hand to him. Her skin is covered in sweat, her clothes drenched. A nurse comes and goes. Miriam doesn't seem to know he's there. All her efforts are going into her breathing, it requires one hundred per cent of her concentration. If anything interferes with it she will stop. Is that what is happening to her? Then she is under a sheet in a cold room. It's the quietest room he's ever been in. But there is somebody else there as well. A man, he is distraught, he keeps putting his head under the white sheet. Perhaps he is a relative of his wife. Miriam. That was her name. Miriam. He wonders where she is.

Ruth is looking at him, really looking at him.

'Where are you?'

He gives her a look as if to say that of course he knows where he is, don't be ridiculous.

'I mean specifically,' she says. 'Where are you?'

'Do you recognize this house? Who lives here?'

246

She must not want answers to them, her questions which come at him so thick and fast. All he can do is look back at her.

'What date is it?'
  'What month?'
  'What's the year?'
  'What's your name?'
  'Christ. What's my name?'
  'Again – where are we? I mean, what city, what country even?'

Her anger gathers in intensity but then loses its ebb and becomes something else that neither of them recognizes. It is like a strange oxygen that they are surrounded by, a mist. There are tears running down his daughter's cheeks. Her eyes are red and sore.

  'You've got dementia, haven't you?'

She reaches for the roll of kitchen paper upright on the table. She blows her nose and dabs briefly at her eyes.

'It's not just the booze, Mike. You haven't got a clue half the time. That weird shit on the plane. Then disappearing off at the airport. That manager at the hotel. He knew all along, didn't he? You must have told him. Doing all that stuff to help you. Booking cars. Always checking on you. He kept calling me you know? Where was I? When would I be back? I thought he was some sort of perv. Which reminds me. Is this why you never drive your car any more? You see, it's all coming together now.'

She taps the side of her head as she says that last part. He laughs. This person is funny. She seems really on top of things.

She shakes her head and looks at him again, then reaches once more for her anger.

'How were you going to do it, Mike? The manager told Isaac you'd rung reception looking for a cab to bring you to Fort Lee. We were wondering about that, Judy and me, we even got the map out. The George Washington Bridge is there, isn't it? Is that what you were going to do? Jump off it? That was Judy's guess. My vote was you'd go for something painless. Like an OD? Or carbon monoxide maybe. But you'd need a car for that. So yeah, the bridge does make sense when you think about it. Judy was right I reckon. She said you'd be unconscious before hitting the water.'

'Well? What about it, Mike?'

'Or was this all a cry for help? A bit of DSH to get attention? Did you have all this planned with your girlfriend Debs? Did you tell her to go up to Judy? At Mum's ceremony and all.'

He laughs again but she is just staring at him. He notices her hair. There's a reddish tinge to it on one side, where the light's on it. This is his daughter speaking to him. Of course he recognizes her, he's not that far gone. He's struck by the fact that she's an adult now. Just like everyone else in the world. But the more he looks at her the more she's a child again. The face of your own child is a riddle like that, flitting back and forth. More tears go down her face, looking out at him fully lost. He wonders what's wrong with her. Why is she crying so much? Did she hurt herself? Perhaps she banged her head or fell off her scooter? He can remember another hospital. He is sitting on a chair holding her when she is just hours old. Miriam is not back from the operating room. Is that where his wife is? It was a difficult birth. Long labour. Instrumentation. There was bleeding afterwards. Some surgery was required. He can feel the small warm weight in his hand, the back of her head, her body running along his arm. The tiny pinched features. The jet black hair and eyes. The jaundiced skin. She needed some sort of light therapy for that. In between sessions he put her on the windowsill of their room, where the sun was strongest. The nurses teased him about it. They don't get through the glass, silly, the ultraviolet rays. You never know, he says back to them, it might help a little. It's warm anyway for her, lying there in a blanket, as yellow as an egg, in the sun.

He laughs.

She leans forward. She is more curious than anything now. Her mother's daughter all right.

'What were you thinking exactly? To just bring me over here and leave me high and dry? Was that your brilliant plan, Mike? Was that it? Am I missing something here, or is that all you've got?'

And now he's not sure if she's telling a joke or not. Just to be safe he laughs anyway.

19

HE IS A familiar face here. The manager knows his order before he has to say anything. He is a young Indian man, the manager, with thick matted dreadlocks. He radiates authority and goodness and is clearly too intelligent for his job. I'll bring it over to you. He looks back at him. The manager has to speak to him again, his voice an ounce firmer. You can take a seat, sir. I'll bring it over to you.

He is one hour early for Ruth. He knows this because it is written down in his journal. Ruth (daughter). 2 p.m. And because there is a clock on the wall behind where the manager is standing. One o'clock. The manager is speaking to him again. Sir. You can take a seat. I'll bring it over to you.

Oh thank you. Thank you.

Three couches form an alcove and he sits in the one facing the window. The place is empty. People here mostly get their orders to go, rushing off then, all business. The door opens regularly, bringing in the cold wind and bits of snow. He leans back against the soft couch and closes his eyes.

He lives in Brooklyn now. Sometimes it might be London, a part of it he's never been to before, which would explain why he doesn't recognize it. Miriam might have moved here, or his mother, or perhaps he is just visiting someone. Strangely he is not particularly curious about this. Sometimes it might even be Dublin, the streets of his childhood, that far-off country. He keeps an eye out for the face of his father, who may be looking for him and who is liable to come out of the crowds at him as he wanders around the streets. In reality of course it is always only Brooklyn and it is a short walk to the coffee shop. (He is never unaccompanied, generally it's one of the children who brings him. Josh or Yoshi or the other one. There's a girl too. The staff know to keep an eye on him.) Neither does he recall the change that brought these cold months which they appear to have entered. It is difficult to imagine that it was ever anything different, the sharp early-morning winds that course down the streets, corralled by the buildings, the banks of snow which isolate the elderly within their homes or strand them on street corners at the mercy of the random helpfulness of strangers.

The manager brings over his bagel. Can I get you anything else? No thank you. By the way, your friend left this behind last night. He places an object down on the table in front of him. He recognizes it and knows what its function is but can't think of the word for it. He's the only person I've seen with one of these, the manager says. It must be like from the '80s.

Yes.

He reaches over to pick the thing up, hoping that physical contact will make him think of the word for it. He holds it and looks at it like some newborn thing. Perhaps the manager will know, but when he looks up at him he is gone, already behind the counter talking to a customer. A man is now sitting on the same couch as Wolf, a few feet away. He looks up at him and their eyes meet for a moment. The man leans over and takes up one of the *New Yorker*s that is on the table.

20

THERE WAS A day where he stood for a lot of photos. Lightning exposing his grin for posterity. It must have been on account of Ruth. That's his daughter, standing over there by those other people who are now looking at him for some reason, waving at him, trying to get his attention. Ruth is the one wearing a black gown, and she is holding one of those things in her hand. Those things that they give out. At the centre of everyone's attention. And now she asks for him to come and he goes to stand there with them all and they nod and smile at him. They are very nice people. Friendly, even a bit deferential to him. One of them slips an arm around his back. It is the girl with the gown. That's his daughter. Her name is Ruth. She is holding one of those things in her hand. Those things that they give out. Banks of photographers focus on them. (In reality it is only one or two and they are pointed in different directions.) Jazz music plays and the young men are wearing bow ties and white shirts.

There is some sort of a dinner afterwards. Or beforehand. Or possibly it is a different day entirely. It takes place in someone's house. It is a nice house, a family house. He doesn't think he has ever been there before, but everyone is so nice.

The walls are covered with pictures that have clearly been drawn by children. They aren't really pictures at all half of them, more like scribbles in crayon, marker, finger paint. Some of them are even framed believe it or not. And there are photographs on the wall of people that must have been taken a century ago, they are dressed like dolls, it is quite funny actually. He laughs and everyone is looking at him. Someone puts their hand gently on his arm. The room is full of people now and they are very pleasant and – he notices this, he keeps noticing this – they really make an effort with him. Perhaps it is a different day entirely. No, the young woman is dressed up again. Her hair is full and thick with a reddish tinge. There is a young man beside her and he seems eager to please, especially when he looks this way. Then all the young people leave and they tell him, No, no, you don't need to go anywhere. You are staying here tonight.

21

YOUR DAUGHTER CALLED. She's running late.

The person speaking to him is a young Indian man with thick matted dreadlocks. The label on his shirt says Manager.

Do you want another coffee?

Yes please.

No, sir, no, it's OK. You sit and I'll bring it over to you. Please, you wait here. Just sit and relax, yeah?

Thank you. Thank you, he says. God, people are so nice in this place. He has already decided that he will come back. Miriam would like it here too. She's always on the lookout for new coffee shops or restaurants that might have opened in the neighbourhood.

And then he is gone.

He picks up one of the *New Yorkers*. There is an image of a vast hill, with an enormous pyramid depicted underneath it. He reads the first sentence over and over but he can't get beyond it. He holds the magazine, but it is in reality an empty posture. He doesn't even read the caption below the image, which summarizes what the article is all about. How the archaeology world has been transformed by technology. How they use enormous ultrasonography machines nowadays. They hang them from helicopters, then fly them over the area of interest. How the layers of the past reveal themselves in the different densities, how they capture in the image the layers of landscape belonging to bygone millennia, the imprints of civilizations we can only guess at, that were once right there in front of your eyes, but now are not even contained within the memory of the world.

When he looks up he sees her in the distance. The view is obscured by the blinding sunlight. And then she is at the door, with a boy. They talk to each other for a while and then say goodbye chastely. She starts to take her leave of the boy but turns back again to say something to him and they both laugh and she pushes on the door to open it and come inside.

He reaches into his jacket pocket and takes out a photograph. It's a Polaroid image that came into his possession at some point, he can't remember when. It's a strange image that he can't explain. He might ask this girl about it, she seems to be on top of things. Maybe she will be able to tell him what the image is. She might even be able to tell him that it is a picture of an apartment on the Upper West Side of Manhattan. One that has just been stripped and is about to be renovated. That the structure is as it was and will never be again, but for now at least is intact and speaks of a specific time that really did exist you know. There is minimal light in the image, seeping through in the background, making the photograph just about possible. There are no people in it and it is a dimly lit scene, like a stage set in between performances, of a play whose very existence is open to question, but is clearly about to start, tense with promise, the fundamental structure still present, still intact, but about to disappear forever. She will in time be able to point to it and tell him that it is this transience which perhaps gives the photograph its permanence, an appearance like nothing on this earth.

Acknowledgements

I REALLY WANT to thank my editor, Bella Lacey, and everyone at Granta; also Mandy Woods. Much gratitude to Faith O'Grady, not only for her support and representation these last few years but also, specifically, for her early review of this manuscript and editorial guidance at that crucial stage; much gratitude again to The Writers Studio in New York, particularly Lisa Bellamy, Peter Krass and Cynthia Weiner, for setting me on the road; and much earlier than this, Sydney Peck, who, when I was 13 or so and had handed him some floridly written, overly long thing, told me he was sure I would have some sort of future in writing. I would like to thank my parents – Vincent and Pauline Duffy – for *everything*, and my sister and brother, Eleanor Ward and Garrett Duffy, for all their support; and lastly, my partner in life, friend and first reader, Naomi Taitz Duffy, also for everything.